Elizabeth M. F

a Healing LOVE

TATE PUBLISHING
AND ENTERPRISES, LLC

Published by Tate Publishing & Enterprises, LLC
127 E. Trade Center Terrace | Mustang, Oklahoma 73064 USA
1.888.361.9473 | www.tatepublishing.com

Tate Publishing is committed to excellence in the publishing industry. The company reflects the philosophy established by the founders, based on Psalm 68:11,
"The Lord gave the word and great was the company of those who published it."

Book design copyright © 2013 by Tate Publishing, LLC. All rights reserved.
Cover design by Junriel Boquecosa
Interior design by Mary Jean Archival

Published in the United States of America

ISBN: 978-1-62994-515-6
1. Fiction / Romance / General
2. Fiction / Romance / Contemporary
14.02.25

DEDICATION

To my Lord and Savior Jesus Christ

CHAPTER 1

CEDAR CREEK, ALABAMA

Dylan McKendricks closed his eyes. "Oh God, I am trying to do what you want me to do. I know you called me to the mission field. I know I am doing your will for my life by starting a church in Australia, but God, I don't want to go back alone. I have been praying for a wife for so many years. I am getting discouraged. I know you have a plan, but I am getting so tired of waiting. I know I need to wait patiently, but God, it is getting so hard." Dylan leaned back on the headboard. Tears streamed unashamedly down his face. "God, I know you have a plan. Please show me your will, and please help me to wait patiently on your answer. God, please. If it be thy will, send me a wife. In your name, I ask all these things. Moreover, I will try to wait patiently and to thank you for all the things you do. In Jesus' name, amen."

Dylan leaned there with his eyes closed, thinking about the last few years of his life. So much had changed since he had first started praying about what God wanted him to do with his life. He slid down onto his pillow, thinking about how evident God's hand had been in his life. *I am so blessed*, he thought. *God has taken me from a little boy, who was not even saved, to a grown saved man whose life is dedicated to mission work.* He laughed a little to himself. If someone had told him five years ago he would be a missionary to Australia, he would have told them they were nuts. Smiling, he gently closed his eyes and drifted off to sleep, his mind racing with all his plans for the next few months. He was going to be very busy.

Nine hours later, a loud knock sounded on his bedroom door.

"Dylan, Dylan! Come quickly, something's happened! You need to come get the phone!"

Dylan abruptly awoke. As he came to, thoughts of his parents or siblings being injured washed through his mind. He rolled quickly out of bed and ran to the phone; he didn't realize it was possible to be so scared of what was going to happen. Even when he had gone to Australia, he was nowhere near so scared. He knew what was to be expected of him. It wasn't completely unknown territory. He had went on several mission trips and survey trips there to figure out what he was going to be doing and where he was going to be at. He picked up the receiver, his hands trembling and his thoughts going hundreds of different directions. *What if Mom and Dad are dead? What if there has been a fire? What if someone has been seriously injured?*

His thoughts went round and round. As he slowly brought the phone to his ear, he could hear Bro. Candsly's children loudly playing down the hallway. From the sounds of it, they were playing Mother May I? The sweet, salty smells of bacon and coffee hung in the air.

"Hello, this is Dylan," he said into the phone. His voice was trembling despite his efforts to keep it steady. "Is everything okay?" Somehow, he already knew that the contents of that phone call would forever change his life.

"Pastor Dylan, this is Molly from the church. There's been an accident. And if there's any way possible, we need you to come back to Australia," she answered.

He closed his eyes, thoughts once again tumbling through his head. *I just got off the plane yesterday evening. The next six months are packed tight with plans. What am I going to do?*

"—but he tried." Molly's voice broke into Dylan's thoughts.

Dylan blinked and shook his head, trying to clear it of thoughts so he could concentrate.

"I'm sorry. What did you say, Molly? What's happened?"

He heard the phone shifting then Molly's voice came back over the line. "Pastor, Matthew fell off the church roof trying to do some repairs this morning. Derrick tried to grab hold of him but couldn't get to him fast enough."

Dylan started drifting off into thought again and jerked himself back to attention. Molly took a deep breath; her tears were evident in her voice. Dylan braced himself for what he knew was coming. Both anger and fear were taking place in his heart.

"When Matthew hit the ground, he landed on a fence post that they had been driving into the ground to help keep the neighbor's roaming sheep out of the church yard. He was killed instantly. There is now no one here capable of looking after the church. In addition, there is no one to speak at his funeral that I feel is trustworthy. I know you have a lot going on, but if it is at all possible, we need you to come home." Molly's voice, edged with emotion, gradually faded.

Dylan slowly sank to the floor, dropping the receiver in his lap. He ran his hands through his black hair and then put his head in his hands. As feelings of hopelessness immediately took hold, his mind was still reeling from what he had just been told. He put the phone back to his ear. Softly, in a voice laced with shock and tension, he spoke into the phone. "I'll be on the next flight headed back to Australia, Molly. I'm sorry. I'll be praying for you guys and his family in the meantime."

He put the phone back down on the hook. He slowly eased his head back against the wall. "God," he whispered, his voice shaking with pent-up emotion. "God, I wanted to come back to the United States so I could find a wife. I am trying to wait on you. Now the only person who I could trust to look after things in Australia is dead, and I am going to have to officiate at the funeral. Matthew was a dear friend. Oh, God, please help Carolyn, Kara, and Jessica as they struggle with his death. They have no family. All they have is the church family. Please help us to be there for them. Thank you for all you do. In Jesus' name, amen."

As he closed out the prayer, his thoughts returned selfishly back to himself. He knew returning to Australia so soon made the likelihood of him finding a wife on this trip slim to none.

I am so tired of being alone. Now it is going to be worse than ever with Matt gone. After all, he was my best friend. Really, he was my only real friend in Australia.

"Oh, God, please help me!" he cried with tears streaming down his face. Was it shameful to want a wife? Was it shameful to be crying because his best friend died?

Somehow, he didn't think so. He sat there, trying to figure out what he needed to do next. Start cancellations or book his flight?

I will book my flight first. Then I'll actually know which meetings I need to cancel.

He slowly stood up and walked back to his room, thinking about Matthew and his family. They had been the first family that had came to the church. After attending the first time, they had not missed a service since. Dylan felt very sad and lonely as he quickly changed clothes and carelessly threw on a brown T-shirt and a pair of denim pants. He shoved on a pair of sneakers, not even realizing through the hazy pain that he hadn't put on a pair of socks. He quickly went to the mirror. *I look terrible!* He noticed the tear tracks running down the side of his face and washed them off with a nearby wash cloth. *Why does everything in my life seem to end in pain?* He absently combed his sleek black hair. *I went to Australia only to find out my grandpa had died, and I could not get back home because of visa laws. I had witnessed to a carload of people who said that they would come to church the following Sunday. They died in a car accident only moments later. I ended up feeling very lonely and discouraged in Australia. I prayed about it, and*

God opened the doors so I could come home. Then when I got home, I hadn't been here twenty-four hours when I got the call I have to go back to Australia and keep the church from folding under in my absence. People honestly have no idea how lonely and time consuming being a single missionary is.

A rough smile crossed his lips as he laid the comb down then quickly sprayed his hair with spray gel. *I am sure going to miss Matt*, he thought, grabbing his keys. *He was always there when I needed him. Now I need to go and be there for his family when they need me.*

He continued to think as he walked down the stairs.

"Is everything okay?" James asked.

He didn't hear or see James and Anna the family friends, who had graciously opened their home while he was in the United States. He continued walking out of the door, got into his truck, and drove off headed for the airport.

Dark-haired James turned to his beautiful wife Anna. "I wonder what's wrong?" he asked.

"I don't know," she replied, puzzlement written all over her face. "I guess if he wanted us to know, he would have told us."

"I suppose you're right, but that phone call sounded urgent, and Dylan was so upset I don't even think he noticed us standing here," James said, turning and going back into the kitchen.

I hope he's all right, she turned and followed her husband into the kitchen.

CHAPTER 2

BOLEMAN, ALABAMA

"Kristina, you can't go through the rest of your life discouraged because you are alone. And you think you always will be." Melony Jason looked at her daughter Kristina. "I know you have longed to get married since you were old enough to know what you wanted. And we raised you that way on purpose. That's the way it should be, but you cannot allow the fact that God hasn't sent him along yet keep you from living your life to the fullest. You have to go on living and serving God while you wait."

Melony stopped and glanced at her daughter. *God, I know you have a plan. However, God, she is getting so discouraged. Please give me the right words to say to her*, she prayed silently, her eyes slowly filling with tears. What was wrong with a twenty-seven-year-old woman wanting a husband? What was God doing in her daughter's life?

I wish there was something I could do to help, she thought, noticing Kristina's Australian flag hanging off the side of her bed. Ever since she was five when a missionary couple going to Australia had come through their church, she had expressed a great burden for those people. She had also expressed a desire to go there and help missionaries as much as she could. The missionary couple that had came through, had told them about the lack of missionaries in Australia. Millions of people without a gospel witness.

A few years later she had done an extensive research on Australia, and had found four different missionaries there. One of them had since passed on. She prayed for these three missionaries every day. It was very inspirational to all her friends and family. Even though the United States needed missionaries of their own, there were actually missionary works in every state. In Australia there were only three that Kristina had been able to locate.

The fact that a twenty-seven-year-old girl who had never been to Australia, could have such a burden for them was slightly overwhelming at times. Melony could remember the first time Kristina had met the Genkins, the very first missionaries they met going to Australia. Kristina had taken a lot of notes from Cassie Genkins, the missionary's wife, and had patterned her life after hers.

Kristina is so loving, submissive, and godly, Melony thought. *She would make a perfect missionary's wife.*

Melony left the room, leaving Kristina alone to pray and think. She was hoping that at least part of this would blow over before Kristina's grandparents arrived that evening. David had invited them in hopes they might be able to boost Kristina's spirits. *I hope she cheers up, especially with her grandparents David and Katie coming and our camp meeting starting tonight.*

Melony walked down the stairs and into the kitchen to prepare supper before her guests got there. In addition, she had to get ready for the meeting. She picked up a carrot and started to slice it. She was making beef stew. Therefore, she would need plenty of carrots. She closed her eyes and paused for a moment, praying that God would give her daughter strength and patience. She smiled softly. Kristina was so beautiful. Tall, willowy, blonde, and blue eyed. She was sure God had someone special for her daughter. *She tries so hard to be a godly, submissive woman*, she thought. *She deserves a good, loving, gentle, kind, godly husband.*

She laughed at herself because of how long the list was and then continued to smile, thinking of all those times she had told Kristina not to make a requirements list for a husband. Now here she was doing it for her. *Nice going, Melony.* Her smile widened into a grin, noticing her husband David sitting at a table. She sat the carrot she was slicing down on the counter. She walked over to the table, wondering what was wrong with her husband as she noticed his slumped shoulders.

She gently slid her chair out and took a seat. She slid her chair in softly and gently reached up and touched his arm. He started violently and looked up at her. She smiled, then immediately noticed the tears streaming down his face. *Oh no! Something has happened.*

He gathered his composure, drawing in a shaky, long breath. He put his hand over hers and closed his eyes, bowing his head. She waited patiently as he composed himself. "I just got off the phone talking with our pastor. Do you remember Brother Ryan and Mrs. Cassie?"

Melony shuddered, dreading his next words. "Yeah, they are the missionaries to Australia that we were trying to arrange for Kristina to go visit for a while." Melony wondered if something had gone wrong with the plans. If it had, though, David wouldn't be all that upset. "They were the very first missionary family in Australia our family had met when we got saved and started attending church. They had stayed with us at our very first house for close to a month due to vehicle problems," Melony recalled.

"Well, they were in a plane headed to the United States from Australia. From the airport, they were supposed to come straight to our camp meeting. That wasn't the only reason they were coming in. But it was the reason they came in so early." David paused and took a deep breath. "Their plane had some difficulties and crashed. As far as anyone knows, there were no survivors."

David's voice caught, and he put his head down on his arms. Melony tensed as tears started flowing down her face. Her heart was heavy and breaking, knowing the pain the missionaries children had to be going through. She took a deep breath. "Is there anything we can do to help the family?" she asked, her voice trembling knowing that question would have been her husband's first words the minute he found out.

"Yes," he replied. "The Pastor said the family needs money to bury them since all of their children are so young, and they were missionaries in a foreign country without a single monetary possession in their name. And another thing, since all their immediate family is deceased, the children need somewhere to stay until something can be worked out."

"Where are the children now?" she asked. Her curiosity was growing.

"They are on a plane to the United States that is supposed to land this evening. They were staying with a trusted family in Australia what time their parents came in to take care of some business. As soon as they found out the plane had gone down, the family they were staying with made arrangements to get them to the United States. They should arrive here sometime around 6:00 p.m. I told the pastor they could stay here for a while." David took a deep breath and looked at his wife.

Melony's thoughts went crazy. *Wow, I have a load of stuff to get done and a rather short time to get it done.* "How long will they need to stay? Or do you know?" She felt slightly sheepish for asking such a question. Many times, when she asked questions like that, David would get upset because he had forgotten to ask.

"The pastor didn't know. It will depend on how long it takes them to make other arrangements for the children. The pastor thinks the maximum time would be a couple of months," he said. He hoped everything would work out and there would be no complications with the children staying with them. He had forgotten that his parents were scheduled to come stay for awhile.

"Okay," Melony said. "I have a lot to get ready. If I remember correctly, they have four children."

"That's right. The pastor said there were three boys and a girl of varying ages. He wasn't sure of exact ages." David pushed away from the table and stood to his feet. "I am going to get the old church van. Bro. Nickels said we could borrow it since all of our children plus the Genkins children will not all fit in our minivan. Kristina could drive her car, but it would make things easier all around if we could all ride in the same vehicle."

He grabbed his coat off the rack hanging by the door, turned, and kissed his wife. "Pastor Nickels said it would be okay to leave our minivan in the church's parking lot. Especially since we are having camp meeting and will be there to check and make sure everything is okay every day," he said. He smiled and headed out of the door.

"Okay, honey. Be careful. I love you," she answered. She followed him out to the garage and watched as he pulled out of the driveway. She watched the minivan disappear around a curve, then she turned and walked back into the house.

Goodness, she thought, grimacing as things she needed to do started coming to her. *I need to clean this house, and then I need to go grocery shopping. However, first of all, I need to find out how old the Genkins children are and what their names are. Hmm. I wonder where I put that last prayer letter they sent. It's usually on it.* Melony went to her desk and started to sort out envelopes.

It has to be here somewhere. She picked up envelope after envelope. *Bro. Jesse Credman's missionary to Brazil. Nope, that's not it. Bro. Jeff Leewood's missionary to Iowa. Nope, that one's not it. Aha, here it is.* She picked up a letter postmarked a few days before, sent from Bro. Ryan Genkins missionary to Australia. It bore signs of having been read often, and Melony smiled, knowing Kristina had devoured every word in that letter and had prayed for them a multitude of times since they had received it in the mail a few days before.

I wonder where they would put that sort of information. She scanned the letter several times from top to bottom. *Here it is,* she thought, looking at the header. Chelsea age thirteen, Derrick age nine, Mason age six, and Samuel age four. *They are so young to have to go through life with no parents.* Tears welled up in her eyes again. It seemed like such a short time ago they had met the Genkins, and they didn't even have any children. They were young and in love with each other and God. And they were on their way to the mission field. Kristina had been five, so it had been twenty-two years ago. She smiled. They had thought they couldn't have children once several years had passed with no luck. Then God miraculously blessed them with four.

It's going to be a long next few weeks, she thought, a grimace crossing her face. She gently bowed her head and closed her eyes.

"Oh, God" she prayed, "please help me through these next few weeks as I try to help these children who have just lost their parents." She lifted her head up and dried her tears. Her schedule had just gotten a lot busier. Now she had to prepare four pallets for the time being so the Genkins would have somewhere to sleep until her in-laws went home. Then she had to go grocery shopping, supper had to be cooked, and they still had to go pick up the children from the airport later that evening. David's parents would be arriving sometime that night, and their camp meeting started at 7:30 p.m.

Oh my goodness, she thought as she slowly headed up the stairs to tell Kristina the terrible news. She closed her eyes for a split second before knocking on the door. *Oh God*, she prayed silently, tears streaming down her face. *You know my daughter is going through a lot right now. Please give me the right words to tell her what has happened. And please, if it be thy will, don't allow this to darken her spirit and discourage her even more than she is already discouraged.*

With tears still streaming down her face and with a prayerful heart, she opened her eyes, raised her hand, and knocked on her daughter's door. Even though Kristina was her daughter, she didn't want to just barge in. As discouraged as Kristina was, she could be praying for her grandparents' coming and camp meeting starting tonight. She could be doing laundry or changing clothes. Melony heard some scuffling, then a brief, shaky "Come in" came from behind the door.

She slowly opened the door, walked to her daughter's bedside, and sat down. Kristina lay back against her headboard, her face showing signs of recent tears and stress.

Melony laid her hand on her daughters arm. *There sure is a lot of tears and sadness going around*, she thought, noticing the empty box of Kleenex lying on its side on Kristina's bed. All of the tissues were in the wastebasket at the side of the bed, wet and crumpled. Melony felt her heart clench at her daughter's pain. No one should have to go through this. However, for some reason, God was using her daughter. He had a purpose; she had to believe that with all of her heart. She took a deep breath and braced herself for the pain that was going to be in her daughter's eyes as soon as she told her about the tragedy.

"Honey," she said, trying not to let her fear for Kristina show through. "I'm afraid I have some bad news."

Kristina sat up, her head pounding. *Bad news? I don't want to hear any bad news today*. She groaned to herself. She looked up at her mom and noticed the tears in her eyes. She could see the nervous frazzle her mom was in and braced herself for whatever her mom was going to tell her. She tried to put her focus solely on her mom. Wow, her head hurt something fierce. She would need to take some aspirin as soon as her mom told her whatever bad news she had. *That's what I get for crying all day*, she admonished herself.

"Sweetheart, I hate to be the bearer of bad news. But a short while ago, we got a phone call from Pastor Nickels." Melony paused for breath, praying silently that Kristina would be able to accept the news of the Genkins' death courageously even though it would hurt a lot. She saw Kristina's shoulders tighten and her hands clench in a dreadful anticipation of the tragic news she knew was coming.

"Kristina, Brother Ryan and Mrs. Cassie got on a plane yesterday headed to the United States. The plane crashed this morning, and there were no survivors," she said, sadness in her voice. Melony watched as first shock, replaced immediately by pain, filled her daughter's eyes, almost immediately followed by tears.

CHAPTER 3

"There were no survivors. There were no survivors." That statement kept churning over and over in Kristina's head. They're gone? Dead? Just like that? No warning? That didn't seem fair. Kristina felt pain unlike anything she had ever experienced clench her heart. And she felt tears welling up in her eyes then overflowing down her cheeks. She closed her eyes against the searing pain that was inside. Her burden for the people of Australia was increasing by the moment. It felt as though it would suffocate her. Now, who was going to tell them? How were they supposed to hear without a preacher? And what about the children? Bro. Genkins' children. What was going to happen to them?

Kristina put her hand against her aching forehead, thinking back over what her mom had said. Were the children even still alive? "Oh God," she prayed. "Please help me." She felt the tears cascading down her face as she tried to regain control of her emotions. She felt so helpless.

"What about the children?" She managed to choke out through all the tears welling in her eyes and the pain that felt like it was going to suffocate her.

Melony watched her daughter's struggle and ached to help her. But there was nothing she could do. Kristina had to work it out on her own. She felt so hopeless as the tears rained down Kristina's face and the pain made her face clench up. She smiled when Kristina asked about the children. That was so much like her daughter, always thinking of others and their pain even through her own. It was always amazing to her how intense her daughter's feelings were toward missionaries and the lost of the world. She thought it was a good thing. But at times it could be a very overwhelming.

"The children were staying with a family in Australia at the time of the accident. They are safe and well. They are actually on a plane headed here. They should arrive here around 6:00 p.m. They don't have any immediate family living. Therefore, for the next few weeks, they are staying here with us. Your dad just left to go get the old church van. Since there are so many of us with them included, the pastor knew we would need a bigger vehicle for all of us to ride in, especially with camp meeting coming up and us needing to transport them daily."

Melony paused for breath, watching the play of emotions traveling across Kristina's face. "I am going to make them some pallets downstairs. Just for temporary use while your grandparents are here. Do you want to help?" Melony asked, thinking that if she gave Kristina something to do, it might help ease her pain.

Inwardly, Kristina groaned. "*Oh, Lord, those children. They are so young. Please help them*," she prayed. She listened as her mom explained the situation, her heart growing heavier and heavier. *God has a plan. I have to believe that*, she tried to convince herself. Make pallets?

"Mom," she said through her tears. "Why do we need to make pallets? There is plenty of room here with me for Chelsea. And my brothers Seth, Abel, Jon, and Dave have plenty of room in their room with their three full-sized beds and a bunk bed for Derrick, Mason, and Samuel in there. Why can't they just sleep with us? That would save us the time of making pallets, and it would have them feel more at home and welcome. I can't even begin to imagine how they must feel right now. Last time they saw their parents, both of them were healthy and happy." Her voice was tense with emotions.

"Even if it cramps us a little bit, we need to think of them and how they must be feeling. They know us just a little bit, so I would think that should make it somewhat easier, but still, everything is going to feel strange for them." Kristina felt small and hopeless to help.

"Of course they can stay with you guys, sweetie. To be honest, I hadn't even really considered that option. I'm going to go downstairs and finish working on supper. When your dad gets back from the church, I need to go to the grocery store and pick up some food. We are going to be feeding a small army." A smile crossed Melony's face. "You may need to watch the stew when I leave. It will depend on how long your dad takes at the church and how long it takes to get the stew done so we can all have supper."

Melony gave her daughter a quick kiss on the forehead and slowly left the room. *Thank you, God*, she thought prayerfully, making her way down the stairs. *She took that a lot better than I dared hope*. She smiled.

Kristina watched her mother leave the room, thinking about how life always surprised you. And so many times, those surprises were bad. She remembered hearing her Grandma Jason say, "When life gives you lemons, make lemonade." She used to think that statement was crazy and meaningless; however, maybe it was not as crazy as she had thought. Life seemed to be throwing her a lot of those lemons recently.

She put her throbbing head in her hands. *I have to take something for this headache.* She stumbled out of bed. She quickly went to the bathroom and took an aspirin out of the bottle she kept in her bathroom cabinet. Every step she took seemed to make her headache all that much worse. *Of all the lousy times to get a headache, I had to get one now*, she thought, grimacing.

She couldn't think straight through all the pain. She went back to her room and stretched out on the bed. She snuggled under the cover feeling a little chilled. "God, please protect Chelsea, Derrick, Mason, and Samuel. Please be their comfort in the days to come," she prayed. She felt the hot, salty, unwanted tears rushing down her face and landing on her pillow. *I am so sleepy*, she thought drowsily as she sank into a much-needed sleep.

CHAPTER 4

CEDAR CREEK, ALABAMA

I hope I can get a plane leaving soon, Dylan thought as he headed down south on Interstate 81. Already his mind was whirling with all the things that needed to come into place before he would be free of obligations so he could head back to Australia. It looked like he would be headed back to Australia alone after all. He felt the blinding, gripping pain tighten around his stomach as he thought of Matthew. He had done so much to help Dylan in the past. Now he was gone, gone without even so much as a good-bye from his friends or his family. Dylan had a hard time wrapping his mind around the fact that Matthew was gone. His best friend in Australia, his only trustworthy member of the church, the only person he had to talk to about the things of life. He was gone. It seemed hard to imagine Matthew anything but happy, healthy, and grinning. That's the way he always had been. Dylan tried hard to control his emotions, but the tears kept flowing, and the pain kept clenching tighter and tighter.

Well, it looked like he should not have come back to the United States after all. Nevertheless, the ticket had been paid for by an anonymous giver, and everything had fallen into place so he could come. Had he misinterpreted what he was supposed to do? Should he have stayed in Australia? Could he have done something to prevent this accident? No, somehow even through all the pain, he knew God had a plan. There was a reason he was in the United States. Whatever the reason was, God had a reason for everything. He pulled into the airport and walked into the office building.

Well, Dylan thought forty five minutes later, he wouldn't have to cancel all his meetings. Seems the first plane headed the Australian direction didn't leave for two days. *I guess I will be able to go to Bro. Nickels's camp meeting after all*, Dylan thought. *Since it starts tonight, I would be able to attend a couple of days.*

He was worried a little bit about being troublesome, so he went to a pay phone and called Bro. Nickels. He made sure it would be okay to put his hotel bill in the name of the church. In addition, that gave him a chance to find out for sure the times of the meetings and where he was going exactly. Bro. Nickels was very excited that he was going to be able to come.

Dylan started down the interstate back toward the Candslys, intending to stay just long enough to grab his suitcase and leave. A few minutes later as he stopped at a stoplight directly off the exit ramp, he wondered how Carolyn and the children were holding up. Losing Matt had to hit his wife and children hard. This had been a huge surprise, a huge bad surprise, he amended thoughtfully. And not just for his family either. It had shocked everyone. No one had time to prepare or really to even process the fact that he was gone yet. Or at least he hadn't. Maybe someone else had came to grips with the fact Matt was gone, but letting go was coming hard for Dylan. Next time somebody offered him a free ticket to the USA, he would second-guess himself before accepting it. But maybe God wasn't done yet. After all, he did still have a few days here in the States before he headed back. There was still plenty of time for God to do something.

Dylan guffawed loudly. Considering his luck, something else terrible would happen. He knew that God wouldn't put more on you than you could bear, but he was sure getting to the end of his rope.

"God, please help me," he prayed, feeling rather selfish. He knew Carolyn and the children needed his prayer and his help, and here he was wallowing in self-pity. He was too busy focusing on his needs and pain to focus on someone else. Dylan grimaced. He was supposed to be a godly example. Loving others the way he loved himself. Being thoughtful and giving whenever possible. And here he was focusing on his problems.

Pfft. Some example I am, he thought. *Here I am praying for myself and not even bothering to mention Carolyn and the children.*

Dylan pulled into the Candslys' driveway. He parked his truck and put his arms on the steering wheel. He let his head rest on his arms and sighed. Today was proving to be one of those awful days when you think you are having a nightmare and will wake up any moment. Real life couldn't be this bad. Dylan smiled at his own wishful thinking and got out of the truck. He closed his eyes for a moment, taking in the silence and hoping the camp meeting he was headed to would revive his spirits.

He took a step toward the house, then the silence hit him. He listened really close hoping to hear some sound, but to no avail; sure enough, it was all quiet. Dylan knew all quiet could only mean one thing. His hosts James and Anna had decided that since he had unceremoniously left this morning, they wouldn't stop their plans and had gone ahead to visit James's parents.

Dylan sighed and walked back to his truck. He sat down and thought for a moment. *I guess I have to wait for them to get back since I forgot to get their cell numbers and no access to the house.*

Dylan closed his eyes. With all the emotions and going to get the ticket back to Australia, he was very tired. He sighed deeply, leaned his head against the headrest, and forced himself to relax. *I might as well try to get some rest. Worrying about how long it's going to take them to get here isn't going to help them get here any faster.* And dwelling on his problems wasn't going to help him none. And besides, there wasn't anything else for him to do. These were his last thoughts as glorious, healing sleep overtook him.

CHAPTER 5

Bang, bang, bang.
Dylan jumped. *What was that?* he wondered, slowly forcing his eyes open. James stood on the other side of the window grinning. Dylan smiled back and sleepily climbed out of the truck. "Hey, James," he said, stretching and taking in the cool, late summer air. He walked with James to the front door.

"Hey, Dylan. It seems you were tired." James grinned at him.

Dylan smiled back. "Yes, I was. Today has been a very long, very emotional day. And it is not even over yet." Dylan felt pain clenching his stomach and realized in all the craziness, he hadn't ate anything all day. His stomach rumbled, and Dylan blushed, knowing there was no way James didn't hear that as loud as it had been. He heard James chuckle as they stepped into the house.

"Are you hungry, son?" he asked, an amused smile lighting his face.

Dylan was so embarrassed. *Why do I always do things to embarrass myself and make me feel so immature?* His cheeks were hot with embarrassment. "Yes, I am," he replied with a sheepish smile. "With everything going on, I am afraid I haven't taken the time to grab something to eat."

James noticed this was the second time Dylan had mentioned something being wrong. *Oh no! Something bad has happened.*

"Dylan, step into the den. Honey, can you please make him something to eat?" he asked his wife Anna, who was standing nearby.

"Sure, sweetheart," she replied, heading into the kitchen.

Dylan stepped into the den and took a seat. *Sure hate to be a bother*, he thought. *They must have ate at his parents' house.* James stepped into the den right after Dylan and took a seat on the couch opposite him. "What's happened?" he asked. He immediately noticed Dylan had tensed up and pain was shimmering in his eyes.

Dylan caught his breath, knowing James was only trying to be a friend. He had no way of knowing how just that question alone would bother him. Dylan felt the tears welling up in his eyes and tried his best to choke them back, but he still felt them sliding down his face. He saw the concerned look on James's face and thought, *Why can't I get a hold of my emotions? He probably thinks I am crazy.*

Dylan swallowed the tears and took a deep breath. "One of my closest friends in Australia, Matthew, the man I left in charge of things that time I was gone, was working on the roof of the church yesterday. He lost his footing and fell, landing on a fence post. He was killed instantly." Dylan paused. His voice was trembling. "I am going to have to go back to Australia. The plane leaves a couple of days from now." Dylan regained control of his emotions and grinned sheepishly at James. "Sorry for the tears. It is painful."

James nodded. "It's okay," he answered the unspoken question in Dylan's voice. "I understand sometimes tiredness and pain can bring you to the point of tears."

Dylan smiled. "I know. I just want to be in better control of my emotions. Seems like every time I go to do something, something bad happens. I don't know why it's like that, but it is," he said.

James nodded sympathetically. "Sometimes life is like that, as unfair as it seems." Are you going to cancel all your meetings or just the ones after you leave?"

Dylan hesitated, not one hundred percent sure how to answer that question. He thought about it a moment. "Unless God changes my mind, I am canceling everything but the camp meeting that starts tonight. Instead of going to that other meeting, I'll just go to that camp meeting until I need to get on the plane. Everyone knows I need some spiritual help. Maybe it's sinful, but I feel so detached. I don't know what's going on. It seems like the pain is growing, and the worse it gets, the farther away from God I feel. I know life isn't supposed to be based on feeling. But I am having a tough time getting through this." His voice was strained.

James smiled hesitantly. "Dylan, I know it's hard. But just remember, it's okay to mourn and to feel pain. Just don't let the pain rule or ruin your life. God is in control. He loves you. And he will never let you down." He noticed Dylan's tense appearance once again and wishing he could help.

Dylan grinned slightly at James's energetic reply. It was obvious that he was putting attention on the fact God would never leave him. "I know that, James, but for some reason that knowledge isn't helping," he said. "I am trying to lean on that knowledge, but its still hard." He was feeling as if he was putting his faith down. Maybe he could get some help at the camp meeting. The more time passed, the more and more he was sure he really needed some reviving.

"Dylan, I know you're a missionary, and you've probably already heard this. More than likely a multitude of times, but I am going to give you something to think about. It's easy to know God is there, and he will never leave you. It's another thing to truly believe it. You can have all the head knowledge in the world and never truly grasp it as heart knowledge." James finished his statement. He noticed he sounded like he was preaching to Dylan. "I am not trying to preach at you," he quickly tried to amend, a sheepish smile on his face.

"It's okay," Dylan said. Then he smiled. "It seems like a very good statement. It defiantly gives me something to think about. I have heard that a lot. But I don't think it's ever really been this real to me. I've never really gave it a lot of thought. I have even said that before, but it never really held any meaning for me."

Dylan sighed. *I really need to think about the meanings of the things I say,* he admonished himself. *Sometimes it seems like I think about all the things that are unimportant too much. And I barely think about the important things. Seriously. That isn't a sign of very much maturity.* Dylan shook his head. *I really need to pay attention.*

The smell of warm, savory, soup broke into his thoughts and captured his attention. It was aromatic tomato soup. *Oh, it smells so good. I hope it's for me,* Dylan thought rather selfishly. "Is that for me?" he asked, his mouth watering. His stomach growled loudly, and he felt his cheeks heat up. *Well, that was embarrassing.*

"Well. I can tell you're hungry," Anna said, a smile on her face as she came through the doorway. A large gray tray was balanced between her hands. Balanced evenly on the tray was a large steaming bowl of hot tomato soup and a plate containing a cheese sandwich fried to a golden crisp. A teaspoon and a napkin lay beside the plate alongside a large tumbler of cold milk. Off to the side of the tray, a saucer contained a huge slice of German chocolate cake.

Dylan eyed the tray, his stomach continuing to growl loudly. *Oh, that looks so good.* He took a deep breath.

Anna smiled. "I hope you like hot tomato soup. You looked tired, and there is nothing like hot tomato soup to hit the spot," she said.

Dylan grinned. "I love hot tomato soup. Thank you so much," he said as she handed him the appetizing tray.

Anna nodded. "It's my pleasure. I hope you enjoy it," she said.

He smiled at her. "I am sure I will. It smells wonderful," he said, his gratefulness shining in his chocolate-brown eyes. He bowed his head. "Dear Heavenly Father," he prayed, tears straining his voice and, against his will, starting to drip down his face once again. The now-familiar pain was gripping his stomach. "God, you know the pain I am feeling. You know how much I love you. How much I long to serve you. You know my heart and the way I am feeling. Please help me to truly believe, you will work all things together for my good. Please help me to believe and truly trust that no matter how long it takes or how much it hurts, you will never leave me or put more on me than I can bear. Please grant me the courage to live through this and the grace to accept it. Thank you for everything you do. Thank you for allowing me to easily find a plane headed toward Australia. Please help the Cartin family as they deal with this awful loss. Thank you for this wonderful family here and for this awesome-smelling food. In Jesus' name I pray." He finished the prayer. "Amen." He lifted up his head, trying to unceremoniously dry his tears. He laughed slightly, noticing James. "Sorry about all the emotion," he said sheepishly.

"It's okay. Enjoy your soup," James said as Dylan ate his first spoonful of soup.

Dylan grinned. "Wow, your wife is a wonderful cook."

"Thank you. She has always loved to cook. She loves anything that has to do with her kitchen. Always has," James replied, his grin widening as he watched Dylan devour the soup. "Slow down, son. There's plenty more where that came from if you need it. You're acting as if you haven't had a good home-cooked meal in a long time. And I know you have. You had one last night," he was getting rather amused at Dylan's lack of decorum.

Wow, this is so good, Dylan thought, relishing the taste. Goodness, but wasn't he hungry. He noticed his bowl was already half-empty. The warm, smooth tomato soup had slid over his tongue like fresh water. He stopped eating and looked up. He noticed James's amused expression and huge grin. "Oh, come on, James," he said. "Cut me some slack. I know I was eating rather unseeingly, but it was so good. It has been a long time since I had tomato soup."

He stopped, noticing James was getting even more amused. "Besides," he paused and grinned back at James. He noticed that with each second, James's grin got wider and wondered how much wider he could grin before it technically became a silent laugh. It was already stretching his face in half. Dylan swallowed hard and took a long drink of milk. It slid over his tongue with all its smooth, cool creaminess, cooling his mouth from the hot tomato soup. "It's not that funny." He completed his sentence, watching as James broke out into full-fledged laughter. *I wish somebody would please tell me what in the world is so funny.*

James doubled over, tried to regain control of himself, he straightened up after several moments, and took deep steady breaths.

Dylan stared at him for a moment, confusion in his eyes. "Okay, what was so funny?" he asked, sounding a little miffed.

James immediately sobered up when he realized Dylan was upset. "I'm sorry." "You just looked so funny sitting there, eating like you hadn't seen a meal in days and eating without a lick of manners." His grin widened, and Dylan sensed that for some reason, he was getting amused again.

"The first thought that crossed my mind was"—James sat down and propped his feet up on the coffee table, tucking his hands behind his head—"no wonder the boy isn't married. He doesn't have any manners." He felt rather sheepish when he realized how it sounded. James noticed Dylan tense up and stopped talking.

Is no manners the real reason I'm not married? Dylan wondered, pain slicing through him at the thought he might have done something to prevent a girl from wanting to marry him. *Stop being silly, Dylan. If you truly lacked manners, someone would have told you before now.* He suddenly started to see the humor in the situation.

"I guess I was eating rather badly," he said, his smile widening to a full-blown grin as he remembered the way he had been shoveling spoonful after spoonful of the hot tomato soup into his mouth. He started laughing as he suddenly remembered his astonishment when he realized his soup bowl was half-empty after only a few seconds. *No wonder he was laughing*, he thought, his laughter still bubbling. *I was eating like a pig.*

He slowly regained his composure and quickly, but this time with manners, finished up the rest of what was on his tray. *Oh, but that German Chocolate cake was so delicious*, he marveled, savoring the last bite.

"Well, James," he said, standing to his feet, a lingering grin on his face and amusement dancing in his eyes. "I need to go get my things and make a few phone calls. Then if I plan to make it to Bro. Nickels' anywhere close to on time, I had better be on my way." He drained the last of his milk.

James nodded and stood. He shook Dylan's hand. "I understand," he said, an answering smile crossing his face. "It was wonderful having you here overnight. I hope you can stay again soon." James noticed the amusement had left Dylan's eyes. It was replaced by such a deep pain, it caused James to blink. "I am so sorry for your loss. Please drive carefully." He walked to the den doorway.

Dylan nodded and tried to smile through the sudden, unexpected blinding pain. "It was wonderful to stay here. Thanks for everything," he managed to choke out, picking up the tray now full of dirty dishes and walking out the door.

James watched him go, a strange sad feeling overtaking him as the reality Dylan was facing now hit him.

CHAPTER 6

BOLEMAN, ALABAMA

Knock, knock.

Kristina awoke. The blinding late-summer-afternoon sunlight was streaming through her window. She blinked to try to clear her blurry eyes and felt the wetness of her pillow as she shifted to her side. She tensed as the memories of a few hours before came back to her in a rush. She tried to steel herself against the pain, but it still hit her all in a rush. She closed her eyes as she felt hot tears stinging in her eyes and welling up in her eyes.

Come on, Kristina. Get a grip.

Knock, knock, came the sound of someone knocking on her door again. Kristina jumped and stumbled up from the bed, hitting her toe on a dresser standing by the doorway. *Oh my. I have to stop hurting myself. I have already hurt myself several times in the past couple of weeks.*

She opened her door, seeing her beaming mom standing on the other side of the door. Kristina laid her head against the door. *What is there to be happy about?* she wondered.

Unlike so many people she met, Kristina realized that a lot of people were just sitting on the church pews, claiming to be Christians, and never doing anything to further the work of God. The people in Australia were dying without a gospel witness because no one would go. It wasn't only the country of Australia, that was in need of missionaries. People could be a gospel witness anywhere, and yet they chose not to do so. The people who had the ability to go were too busy going about their daily lives to work on something so important as the lost people dying without Christ. Why would no body go? Why did most Christians sit on the church pew's saying that they are living in the last day's and yet they act like they have forever oblivious to sinners, and eternity alike. Not bothering to spread the news that Jesus died for their sins and all they had to do was accept the free gift of salvation.

"God please send someone," she prayed briefly.

Kristina scowled. Well, her mom might be happy for whatever reason. But as far as she was concerned, there was absolutely, positively no reason to be happy. She looked back up at her mom, who, for some reason, was now grinning all the wider.

"Hey, sweetheart, can I come in?" she asked, breezing right past Kristina.

Oh, brother. Something else bad must have happened. And she's pretending to be happy to try to throw me off track and make me feel better. Kristina groaned and then let out a long sigh and hobbled over to her bed, noting along the way how bad her toe was throbbing. She took a seat on the edge of her bed and smoothed the huge lump of red, white, and pink coverlet lying in the middle of her bed.

Her mom walked through her room, sliding a pair of boots with her foot out of the way. She sat down on the edge of Kristina's bed and turned toward her daughter, her light-green eyes sparkling with pleasure and a beaming grin on her face.

Kristina stared at her mom in astonishment, wondering if she had gone insane. *Everything is going wrong, and my mom is happy?* "Mom, what's wrong?" she asked, puzzlement obvious by her tone.

Her mom's eyes softened, and she smiled softly at her daughter, taking her hand. "Kristina, honey. I know everything is going wrong right now. But I promise, what I have to tell you is not bad. It's wonderful," she said.

Kristina looked at her mom, quickly noticing that her mom was genuinely happy and seemed to think that whatever she had to tell her was honestly something exciting and fun. She looked at her mom and tried to smile. Despite of herself, she was still feeling the stinging pain of loss. *Goodness. They meant a lot to me. But as much as this hurts, you would think that I was related to them in some way.* "Okay, Mom," she said. "What's the news?"

Melony smiled back at her. "Well," she said, excitement tingeing her voice. "You know your dad's parents were coming for a visit, and since we don't get to see each other much, they were going to stay a couple of weeks. But guess what?"

Kristina watched her mom's excited movements and heard the excitement in her voice. "Well, I am not sure what it is, but whatever it is sure has you excited." She watched her mom's face light up.

"Well, my parents are coming for a visit too. They will be here for a couple of weeks as well," she said.

Kristina looked at her mom, astonished at what her mom had just said. Her mom's parents were coming. *Wow, that is news. I don't remember ever even meeting my mom's parents. Mom was right. This is really exciting.* She looked up at her mom and grinned. "That is exciting," she said, her face starting to light up. *I am finally going to meet my mom's parents.*

Melony watched her daughters' face light up, and she smiled. *Finally, I get to deliver her some good news.* She watched Kristina as her excitement started to increase. Ever since that morning when she had to tell Kristina that her most loved missionaries had been killed in a freak accident, she had longed to be able to give Kristina some good news. Her daughter had so much to bear. She had such a burden for the people of Australia. It slightly scared her. Kristina would lie for hours on her bed. She would sit beside her bed with her head bowed for hours, crying out to God to save the Australian people. Melony smiled. Out of all the people Kristina could have started praying for and came under a burden for, it had to be the Australian people who she had heard so little about. Melony felt a little afraid at what a burden like this meant.

God must have an awesome plan for her daughter's life. He had made the thought of someone dying without Christ so real to her that she couldn't get away from the fact there was so many people in the world that were dying without Christ that had never heard. It didn't seem to bother her as much that there were people that had never heard; even though it was obvious, it bothered her. She really dwelled on the fact that the people who hadn't heard were dying without Christ.

She smiled as she saw God's hand working in her daughter's life. It was obvious God had a great plan for Kristina. Melony just wondered what. As much of a burden as Kristina had, it wouldn't have surprised her in the very least if she ended up a missionary's wife or a preacher's wife.

Melony stood up. *I will leave her here to get ready to go to church. She probably needs to process the fact that she is going to finally meet her grandparents. She has had such a hard time of it.*

Melony stood up and headed toward the door, pulling a pink T-shirt out from under the bed with her foot as she did so. She smiled as she bent and picked it up. She threw it in the dirty clothes hamper and turned to her daughter. "I am going to go back downstairs. Supper is done, and it is five fifteen. We have to go get the Genkins children off the plane soon. Your grandparents should be here anytime, and we have the camp meeting starting tonight. You might want to change clothes soon. I love you." She walked out the door.

Kristina watched her momma walk out the door and walked over to her dresser to grab her T-shirt. She had never met her mom's parents. They had always lived several hours away, and the two families had never made an effort to meet each other until recently. *I don't feel like getting all dressed up. If I feel better after a while, I will change into something nicer. This is so exciting*! she thought, her actions showing her excitement. *I can't wait to meet them. It is going to be such fun.*

She pulled a soft light-pink cardigan out of her top dresser drawer and started to put it back in. She paused and looked at it. *I think I will wear this cardigan. It is a lot nicer than a T-shirt without being too dressy.* She took off the old green pajama top she was wearing and pulled her white T-shirt down. She quickly pulled the pink cardigan on and smiled at the feeling of the sleeves. *This is so soft. I always loved this shirt. It is so warm, and it feels so good.*

She pulled out the next drawer down and got out a long white jean skirt. *It is a solid color, it's serviceable, it's appropriate for church without being to dressy.* She put it on and walked over to her mirror. *Looks reasonable*, she thought, noticing that her skirt was caught on the side of the bed and moving it off. She grabbed a comb lying off to the side of the mirror on a brown stand and quickly combed through her hair. *Ugh. My hair is so full of tangles*, she thought as the comb caught and jerked her head down. She groaned at the pain and quickly worked all the tangles out. She laid the comb back down and grabbed a pair of knee-highs out of the drawer. She sprayed her hair with hairspray and slipped her pink dress shoes on. She walked out of her room and went into the bathroom.

A few minutes later, she walked down the stairs and into the kitchen, the smell of frying meat and stew filling the air and the warm, enhancing smell of coffee drifting up the stairs. She walked into the kitchen and stopped in the doorway. An older man and woman she had never seen before stood at the table drinking her momma's favorite lemonade. She watched as her mom talked to them as if she had known them her whole life. She took a step forward right as they looked up.

The woman smiled as tears welled up in her eyes. The man just stared as if he had never seen a girl before.

This must be Mom's parents, she thought, right before a bombardment of thoughts hit her. *What if they don't like me? What if I am not what they expected? What if...what if... what if?*

What if's kept running through her head as she took another step forward. She watched as the man and woman turned toward her and started walking to her. *What am I going to say? What are they thinking? Kristina, get a grip!* she shouted to herself.

The woman reached her and, smiling, reached up and took Kristina's hand. "Hi, Kristina," she said. "I am your grandmother Chelsea. I am your mom's mother." With her voice choked with emotion, she reached up to give Kristina a hug, making sure to give Kristina plenty of time to pull away.

Kristina smiled at her grandma. "It's nice to finally get to meet you," she said. She put her arms around her grandma and squeezed, noticing the sweet warm vanilla smell and the softness of her grandmother's voice. She felt tears welling up in her eyes. It was so nice to finally know who her grandma on her mom's side is. She had longed to meet her since she was old enough to realize that they weren't around. She felt her grandma's arms squeeze around her as she stepped back.

"I am so happy to see you. I have wanted to meet you for so long," Kristina said. It took a minute, but then her grandma burst out in tears. She looked over at her mom, and with tears streaming down her face, went to her and put her arms around her.

I wonder what is going on, she mused as she stepped forward with the intentions of giving her grandpa a hug. She spoke up in a small voice. "Hi, Grandpa." She watched as his eyes filled up, and he took a step toward her.

That was all it took. She threw her arms around him and gave him a hug. She heard her dad come in through the back door, and his voice boomed out through the house. "Jonathon, Chelsea. It is so nice to get to see you guys," he said, coming into the room.

Kristina smiled and looked at her mom. "Mom?" she said.

"Yes, honey?" her mom said, turning toward her.

"I am going to go outside and take a short walk and try to clear my head."

"Okay."

"What's the matter with her?" She heard her grandpa ask as she started out the door.

"She has had a lot to deal with today. One of the missionaries she prayed for every day that she actually wanted to go visit was killed in a plane accident this morning. It really bothered her. She has had a burden for the people of Australia, which is where those missionaries were going, ever since she was seven years old. She has done an extensive research on the people and the missionaries there." She heard her mom saying as she walked out the door.

Kristina paused as she closed the door behind her. *Mom really does understand what I am going through*, she thought with a smile, seconds before the pain hit. "Oh God," she prayed, "please help me to serve you. Please help ease this pain."

CHAPTER 7

CEDAR CREEK, ALABAMA

Dylan closed his eyes as he walked into the room where he had stayed the night before. *Good grief. This room is an absolute mess.*

He noticed the clothes strewn all over the room. Pants lying on the top of the dresser. Shirts and ties lying half out of his suitcase and all over the floor. He sighed. *Goodness. I need to learn to clean up after myself. I wish I had thought about the fact that I would be leaving soon, and I would have to pack it all back up anyway last night when I made this mess.*

He had come to the room last night and just threw stuff all over, trying to find a clean pair of socks that he had, for whatever reason, put in the bottom of his suitcase. *What on earth was I thinking?* he wondered. *Putting socks in the bottom of my suitcase. That was rather senseless.*

He grabbed his suitcase and decided he would just throw the stuff in there. The stuff was already wrinkled up from where he had thrown it all over the room the night before.

Pfft, he said to himself. There was the blue T-shirt he usually wore as an undershirt. He had thought he hadn't packed it. He laughed at himself. *What is the matter with me? I mean, for crying out loud, I felt a lot better yesterday than I do today. I had no reason to be upset yesterday.*

He moaned to himself and grabbed the shirts that were hanging off the bookshelf.

Wait, hanging on the bookshelf? How did those get there? he wondered, shoving them in the bag. He quickly shoved all the remaining clothes into his bag and practically ran out the door. On the way out, he looked at his watch. *I have to get going*, he thought, noticing that it was two, twenty-five. He had to be at Bro. Nickels' which was a couple hours away, at 5:00 p.m. He had promised Bro. Nickels he would help set the tables up in the fellowship hall before the meeting since all of Bro. Nickels' members were busy and wouldn't be able to be there until 6:00 p.m., and the service started at 7:00 p.m.

I hope this helps get my mind off this blinding pain, he thought, all the while wishing that like physical pain, he could curl up around it, and it would go away. The thought of being stuck in Australia alone again was almost as bad as the pain of losing Matt.

I guess the true pain of losing Matt will really hit me when I get to Australia as he isn't there. Right now, it's a head knowledge. When I get there and he's not there, I will be forced to face the reality that he's not there. And he's not coming back. He felt tears stinging the back of his throat. He swallowed hard and stepped off the stairs into the hallway.

He quickly walked through the hallway and out to his truck, noticing the sounds of Ryan's children playing. Gosh, but they were loud. It sounded like they were killing each other. Screaming and hollering. He smiled as he remembered all his brothers and sisters and wondered if they had ever been that loud. He started grinning. They probably had.

He threw his suitcase into the back of his truck and shut the door. He leaned up against his truck and laid his head on the hood. Goodness, he was tired. He guessed it was from all that running around he had been doing. God must have sent him here to make him tired. He smiled to himself. *That is ridiculous, Dylan.* Then it hit him. *My feelings change so quickly and easily. As long as I don't think about Australia, having to go back there alone, and Matt's death, I am fine. But if I even so much as think about them, then I get really sad, and a blinding pain clenches my heart.*

He thought about it for a moment, his amazement growing as he realized how quickly your feelings could change based on what you are thinking about and doing. He felt the pain start pulling him down again, and he decided it would be best for him to find a place to pray and be alone.

He went into the house and told Anna he would be back in a few minutes; informing her that he was going to take a walk. Her eyes and face filled with understanding, and she gave him a soft smile. "Okay, Dylan," she said, watching him turn and walk out the door. *I hope he gets a hold of God and will let go of his emotions and allow his tears to flow freely for a while,* she thought as she watched him close the door behind him.

CHAPTER 8

Dylan stepped out the door of the house and walked to his truck. He opened the door of his truck and picked up the small clear bottle of store-bought water the airline had given him. He pondered where he was going to walk. *I guess I can do through the woods and walk down to the lake. That would be a peaceful place to be alone and pray.*

He felt slightly silly as he walked, realizing that so many people thought a man wasn't supposed to cry. *Yikes, I hope that when I pray and think about it and read my Bible, God will give me some peace and help ease some of this pain and emotion.*

He walked down to the lake, noticing the clean air, the wonderful scent of fresh pine, and the fresh smell of the water. He noticed the sounds of the birds twirling in the trees and the rush of the water flowing along the lake bed. He heard the sound of squirrels chattering and the soft whoosh as a deer bounded off into the forest. He smiled at the peacefulness.

How could anyone behold all of this and still not believe that God created it? It was so beautiful and so peaceful. Everything was quiet. Nature's sounds were relaxing. He smiled and walked over to a log he noticed down next to the lake. He sat down and looked out over the lake and the bluish white of the water as the sun reflected off it. In addition, the soft smell of the summer afternoon relaxed him.

He bowed his head and started to pray. "God, I know I have asked this of you a lot today. However, I am in a lot of pain. God, you are my creator. You love me, and I love you. Please help me to live life to the fullest. God, the pain of losing Matt is awful." He felt the hot, scalding, salty tears well up in his eyes, and instead of choking them back as he had been doing, he let them flow. Sobs overtaking him, he put his head in his hands and continued to pray in a voice strained with tears and pain. "The pain is so bad, it feels like it is ripping me apart. God, outside of you, Matt was all I had. He was the only person there I could talk to. He was the only person to lean on. God, he meant a lot to me. I feel so horrible, but the thought of the fact Matt is gone hurts nothing compared to the pain of going back to Australia with literally no one." He paused, trying to regain a little bit of control. It didn't seem like the pain should be this bad. He used to think it was so crazy that people would be upset over people dying who they were not related to. He also used to think that men who would not take on single missionaries for support were silly. Sure, it might be God's will for a man to go to the mission field alone, like it had been for him, but then again, being alone there had been the worst experience of his life.

He grimaced and allowed the tears to have free course down his face. He tasted the salt of the tears and felt the hot tears sliding down his face and stinging his eyes. "God, I know that you love me. But I am having a hard time seeing that right now. Help me to understand and truly believe that you will work all things together for my good and for your glory. Please give me the grace to go back to Australia alone. And please, if it be thy will, allow me to find a wife soon. Please give me faith and patience to serve you while I wait. Help me to always be found doing your will. In Jesus' name, amen."

He lifted his head and gazed at the water the tears still slipping down his face. He felt slightly embarrassed at all the emotions. However, he would rather be emotional than completely detached. He wondered if he would ever find a wife then grinned sheepishly at his own thoughts. *The Bible plainly says to believe that he will answer you. And here I go praying a prayer, and I no more than get it out of my mouth then I doubt that God will do it.*

He groaned and watched a couple of ducks swimming nearby. He picked up his Bible and started to read. God knew what he needed, and maybe he could find it in the Bible. After all, that was God's only written words to mankind. He wondered where to read. He opened his Bible to the book of Philippians. He smiled as he found the verse that read, "With God, all things are possible." Yep, that was exactly what he needed to read.

He closed his Bible and gazed out over the mountain and across the lake. He looked at all the beautiful colors in the flowers surrounding the trees and smiled. Somehow, it seemed that just when you need something from the Bible, the answer was right in front of you.

Dylan pondered this for a moment then bowed his head. "God, please help me to trust that you can do all things. Even send me a wife when in man's eyes, God, even sometimes in my own eyes, it seems impossible." He lifted his head and gazed around him once again, noticing the beauty of the land. He stood up and stretched then slowly walked back to his truck, thinking about all the things that had went on in his life in the past few months. Seems his whole world was bound and determined to come crashing in.

He felt slightly sheepish as little Caddy, one of Brother James's daughters, came up to him and said, "Have you been crying? Is everything okay, Bro. McKendricks?"

He tried his best to smile. Seems praying and crying had helped the pain. He grinned as he realized that the pain had eased. The knowledge was still there. However, the gripping pain had eased. He looked up toward the heavens. "Thank you, God," he whispered to himself.

"I'm sorry, Bro. McKendricks. What did you say?" came a little voice by his side.

He started and looked down at the little girl standing beside him. "Oh, I'm sorry," he said. "I was thanking God for being so good to me. And to answer your question, yes, I have been crying, and no, everything's not okay right now. But with time and God's help and grace, I will get through it okay. No need for you to worry." He smiled down at the worried little face. *I hope I eased her fears. I do not want the little one to worry about me.* He watched as she put her arms around his legs.

He picked her up. "I'm okay, sweetheart," he added, noticing that she seemed to be even more worried about him.

"I think you are not okay," she said, her little five-year-old face filled with all the worry she could possible have.

He smiled gently at her and squeezed her shoulder. "I am okay. I just found out some sad news, and it made me cry," he said, looking at her. She had the prettiest blonde ringlets and soft brown eyes.

"Oh, sad things make me cry too," she said happily. She practically jumped out of his arms and ran off to play. He grinned, feeling a little bit confused. Leave it up to a child to say something he didn't understand. Who knew why it made her happy that he was sad when sad things happened? He shrugged his shoulders then walked to his truck and threw the empty water bottle into it. He laid his Bible on the seat and walked into the house. He was hoping to use the phone. He still hadn't called and canceled his meetings. And if he were even going to attempt to make it to Bro. Nickels' on time, he would need to go soon.

He noticed the grass seemed to be drying out, and he could see and hear the laundry flapping in the wind. Apparently, Anna liked to hang her laundry out to dry. That would explain the wonderful springy, outdoorsy smell that had been in his sheets. He knew that he hadn't ever smelled any soap that smelled that good.

He walked into the house and heard James and Anna talking. He turned and walked down the hall and into the dining room where the telephone was. The dining room was a pale silvery blue. The window was raised, and the curtains were flapping in the wind. The smell of fresh-baked chocolate chip cookies caught his attention. *Yum, those smell good*, he thought. He walked across the dark, beautiful hardwood floor, taking extreme care not to scuff it up with his dress shoes. He saw his bare ankles as he reached back into his pocket to get his wallet so he could call the pastors whose meetings he was scheduled to attend.

Wait. What? He paused a moment and reflected on what he had just seen. Had it been bare ankles? He pulled his pant leg up, and sure enough, no socks. *Goodness, I was in such a big hurry this morning to get to the airport, I didn't even put on any socks.*

He picked up his pen and wrote a quick message on the palm of his hand: "remember to put on socks." He pulled his wallet out of his pocket and found the sheet of paper that had all his scheduled meetings written down. He kept it all on a couple of sheets of notebook paper along with pastors' names, phone numbers, and addresses to the churches. He scanned the list. It would be well over one hundred cancellations. He was scheduled to be very busy the next couple of months. Oh well. He would be busy all right, but not with meetings like that. He would be busy taking care of Matt's funeral, fixing the roof on the church, taking care of both his and Matt's duties, and trying to comfort Carolyn. He groaned. The list kept on growing. Every time he thought about it, the list was longer. He would need to try to rest some before he got on that plane to Australia. Because once he got there, there was not going to be any resting. He would be working, working, working.

He thought about it for a few minutes then decided he might just go to the second day's morning and night services at Bro. Nickels. That would give him several hours to rest, and he would not be missing a whole lot of preaching. Normally during the daytime, they just had a lot of singing and a little bit of preaching anyway.

He glanced down at his clock. It was three forty-five. He needed to get on the road. He picked up the phone and dialed the first number. Close to an hour later, he put the phone on the cradle for the last time. He sighed. *Gosh, making all those cancellations took a long time. I am going to be late, but there is nothing I can do about it.* He grimaced. *They were all so nice about it though. I guess that's a good thing.*

He raised his head and looked up at the ceiling. "Thank you, God, for giving the people understanding about me having to cancel the meetings. God, please allow me, if it be thy will, to raise some support at this meeting up at Bro. Nickels'. Please help me be a blessing to those people. Please bless all the pastors of the churches I just had to cancel the meetings for. They were very understanding and thoughtful. Please grant me traveling grace, and allow me to make good timing on the road. In Jesus' name, amen."

He picked up the sheets of paper and stuffed them back in his wallet. He walked into the kitchen where James and Anna were talking.

"I hate to interrupt, but if I plan on getting to Bro. Nickels' anytime tonight, I need to go." He said and then smiled over at them.

"It's okay, Dylan. Travel safely. Our prayers are with you," James said.

Anna nodded, speaking up, "Yes, Dylan. It was wonderful to have you here. It was such a blessing to get to know you. I hope you get there safely and that you get some spiritual help what time you are there."

Dylan smiled at her. "Thank you, and thanks for your hospitality," he said. He walked to them and shook their hands. "Thanks once again for everything." He turned and walked out the door feeling sadness wash over him, at leaving these humble people. He heard James behind him and felt him place his hands on his shoulder.

"Dylan, our prayers are with you. Please keep us updated," he said.

Dylan smiled, feeling loved for the first time in a long time. "I'll be praying for you guys too, and I will try my level best, to keep you updated," Dylan said. Then he turned and strode out the door.

He climbed in his truck and started the engine, buckling his seat belt. "Please help me drive safely, God, and please help the Candslys." He opened his eyes, smiled, and pulled out of the driveway.

CHAPTER 9

MILESTONE, INDIANA

Megan closed her eyes and felt like screaming. What was up with brothers? Oh gosh, did they ever annoy her. She should know too; she had eleven of them. No matter that six of them had moved out, there were still five of them still living in the house. She groaned. Who knew when the others would move out too.

She moaned to herself gently, closing the door to her bedroom behind her. She sat down on her purple-covered bed. Everything in her room was purple. Her favorite color was purple. Megan heard her brothers rowdily running down the stairs into the kitchen. Maybe Mom would find them something to do, and then they would leave her alone. She laughed. Yeah. That was not going to happen. As soon as they had their snack, right back to her room they would be coming. Oh, how she missed her brother Dylan. He had always made the other boys leave her alone so she could concentrate. And he would sit there outside her door and make sure they left her alone.

She heard one of her brothers quickly racing up the stairs. "Meg! Hey, Meg!" he shouted before he even reached her door.

She looked up at her door, anger clouding her face. She was tired of her brothers hollering at her. She got up and walked to the door of her room, stepping across a mountain of clothes she had apparently forgotten to take down to the laundry room. *Mom sure wouldn't be too happy about that*. She opened the door and glared at her brother Samson as he rounded the last stair. "Would you please stop hollering at me before you even get to the door, Samson? Acting like that is not very gentlemanly," she said.

She laughed slightly to herself. Who was she kidding? Her nineteen-year-old brother was not a gentleman. He liked to claim himself as one, but he really wasn't. "What did you want?" she finally ventured to ask as he glared at her, anger shimmering beneath the surface of his eyes.

"What do you mean it's not very gentlemanly?" he asked, his voice bordering anger.

"I just meant that everyone knows you are not a gentleman," she replied.

He watched her a minute, assessing everything that she did. "Mom wants you to come downstairs," he stated, anger simmering in his voice. He turned and walked back down the stairs, anger obvious in every step.

Megan turned and went back into her room. Her mom wanted her. That was different. Usually this time of day was the family's free time. But oh well. She grabbed a pair of tennis shoes and slipped them on her already-socked feet.

Then she quickly went down the stairs, heading into the living room. She could hear her brothers loudly debating over something and realized that the whole family was gathered in the living room.

Oh no... That could only mean a couple of things. It could mean something wonderful was going to happen, something wonderful had happened, something bad was going to happen, or something bad had already happened. She groaned to herself. With her luck after the way she was feeling today, it would be one of the latter two. She smelled bread baking and smiled. Seems her mom decided that they were going to have sourdough bread for supper after all.

She walked into the living room and quietly assessed the scene before her. Her brothers were seated Indian-style on the floor in a semicircle around her parents, loudly discussing something about her brother Jim's motorcycle. Apparently, all had different opinions about it. Her sisters were seated beside her parents on their long burgundy couch. She sat down in the empty seat beside her sisters.

Immediately, her dad cleared his throat and spoke up, placing the newspaper he had been reading on a side table. "All right, now that we are all here, your mom and I have some good news for you." He smiled and took her mom's hand.

Megan breathed a sigh of relief. *Whew, seems it's going to be something good. So much for my silly premonitions.* Megan smiled at her own thoughts and turned her attention back to her dad.

"We just got a phone call from Bro. Nickels. If you guys will remember, I told you we couldn't go to his camp meeting this year because we were tight on money. Well. He told the church about it. And they raised a special offering to pay our way. We are going after all." He smiled as the boys broke out into cheers and started shouting at each other about what they were going to get to do.

Megan's heart jumped. *Yes! I so wanted to go*. She had been so disappointed when her parents had to tell them that there was no way they could afford to go. She softly laughed and then gasped as she remembered a phone conversation with her brother Dylan a few weeks before.

"Mom and Dad!" she exclaimed, happiness shining in her face and voice.

"Yes, honey, what is it?" her mom replied, slightly worried something might have upset her.

"Dylan will be there," she answered breathlessly.

Her dad stopped talking to her brothers and turned toward her. The whole room fell in a total silence. "Oh... Yes, he will," her dad said, then grinned. "I had completely forgotten about that."

Her mom started crying, and her brothers' shouts increased as they shouted they were going to see Dylan. It had been so long since they had seen him, and oh, how everyone had missed him.

Megan gently smiled as the happiness in her heart started overflowing, and then the tears came dripping silently down her face. She gently wiped them off her face and spoke up.

"Well. Since we will have to leave tomorrow, I will go ahead and pack my stuff up."

"Okay, honey," her mom responded. "We all need to go pack just in case things need to be washed. And we will have to leave pretty early in the morning." She pointed the boys to their rooms. They all clambered up and ran to their rooms, their boots stomping on the stairs and creating an awful racket.

Megan smiled. Leave it up to her brothers to sound like elephants going up the stairs. Megan followed her brothers up the stairs, keeping a straight face until she got to her room. Then she broke down in sobs. Oh, how she missed Dylan. And she was going to get to see him soon. That thought spurned her into action.

She grabbed her suitcase out of the closet and went through her clothes in a frenzy. It was a good thing she kept her clothes washed, unlike her brothers, who probably had all their dress pants in the hampers so on Sunday mornings they could look at Mom and say, "But we don't have any dress pants clean. We will have to wear jeans." She smiled. As if her mom didn't figure out that trick a long time ago. She picked up a soft pink outfit her brother had bought for her, and a huge smile crossed her face. She would wear this down there. Maybe he would already be there.

CHAPTER 10

BOLEMAN, ALABAMA

Kristina walked out by the garage, her gaze scanning the area around her. The wind was swirling the leaves up and around. The sound of the wind whistling through the trees was both relaxing and refreshing. She felt the cool breeze blowing across her skin as she took a seat on the bench out behind her parents' garage. The crickets were chirping nearby, and the bullfrogs were loud down by the pond. The crisp smell of the late summer night was relaxing as she leaned her head back against the garage and closed her eyes. She took several deep breaths, clearing her head and trying to clear her thoughts.

Why did Brother Ryan have to die? she wondered. He was one of the only missionaries she knew of in Australia. God had given her such a burden for them. She had thought it was so she could go and help Brother Ryan, but apparently, it wasn't. There must be some other reason. Maybe it was to pray for Australians, but somehow, she knew that wasn't all. God had a plan for her that involved Australia. She had never completely understood the burden she held for the foreign county, having grown up in the United States she was well aware of the need for missionaries in America. But at least American's had preachers and missionaries in every state that she knew of personally. In Australia there were little to none. Maybe at the upcoming meeting she would meet a missionary she could go and help. At least, she hoped to find another missionary to Australia that was very important to her. A specific missionary to pray for and hope that God would lay his hand upon and bless abundantly and beyond what they ever asked or thought.

Kristina smiled. That is what God was good at. Blessing abundantly above and beyond what people thought. She remembered all the stories Brother Ryan and Mrs. Cassie had told about how they had prayed for things, and the next thing they knew, that thing would happen and abundantly more than they asked for. Kristina had always felt that her prayers played a part in all those things happening, but she guessed she would never truly know until she got to heaven. She could smell the warm smell of her mom's stew wafting out the open widow and the low dialogue of her parents and her grandparents. Her *grandparents*. She smiled. It had sure been wonderful to meet them. She had always had an incredible longing to meet them. In the beginning it had been very awkward, but that had passed after a couple of minutes. Maybe after a while, she would feel just as comfortable around them as she did her dad's parents.

I sure hope it's not as awkward this time, she mused. She scanned the area around her, noting all the beautiful flowers blooming out by their house. She smiled. Her mom had a habit of always planting flowers at the oddest times. Here it was late July, and her mom had flowers planted. She could smell their scent from where she was seated. Pansies had a tendency to be smelly, at least in Kristina's opinion. She glanced around, noticing her next-door neighbor kissing her husband good-bye as he left for his late-shift job.

A pang shot through her heart. *I want a husband. The Bible says a man that findeth a wife findeth a good thing. So…wanting a husband cannot be wrong*, she mused.

It must be me. I must not have a husband because something is wrong with me.

Somehow through all her musings, it never occurred to her that there might not be anything wrong with her. It might just be the fact God had not brought the right man along yet. She glanced up as her mother stepped out onto the steps. "What is it, Mom?" she asked.

"I have supper ready," her mom responded, stepping back into the house.

Kristina nodded and slowly stood up. Maybe God would see fit to bring her a husband after she found out where her burden for Australia was leading her. God had a purpose for everything. Eventually, God would tell her what he wanted her to do. She walked back into the house, slowly closing the door behind her. Everyone was seated around the large family-sized table. The tantalizing smell of stew got better and better the closer she got to the table. A huge black pot of stew was sitting in the middle of the table next to a platter of grilled cheese sandwiches. Kristina smiled. It was her favorite meal. Somehow, whenever she felt bad, her mom always did something to make her feel better. Plus her favorite meal was often served when they had guests because it went a long way. Her other set of grandparents should be arriving anytime.

About that moment, a knock sounded on the door. David looked at his daughter and nodded at the door. They all knew who it was, and she was already up and nearest to the door. She walked over to the door and opened it.

CHAPTER 11

INTERSTATE 81, ALABAMA

Dylan continued down the interstate, his mind whirling. All of a sudden, the phone broke into his thoughts. He picked it up, flipping it open in one fluid motion. "Hello," he said into the receiver.

"Hi, Dylan, this is Bro. Nickels. I was wondering, since you were going right by the airport, if I could request a favor of you."

Dylan started in astonishment. What in the world could he do to help Bro. Nickels? Well, whatever it was, he would be happy to do all he could to help. "Sure, I'll do whatever I can."

"Well, I just got off the phone with one of my church members. I am sure you have probably heard about the tragic accident involving Brother Ryan and Mrs. Cassie Genkins?" Bro. Nickels stated, taking a breath.

"No, I can't say I have," Dylan answered.

"Oh," Bro. Nickels said. "They were killed in a plane accident this morning."

A sharp pain shot through Dylan's heart. They were dead. Why was everyone dying? What was God trying to prove to him? Now there were even more people in Australia who needed a missionary. Why didn't more people go? Dylan could feel the roots of bitterness starting in the corner of his heart, and he tried to suppress it. "Aw. I'm sorry to hear that," Dylan answered, feeling as though he was talking from miles away. "That's terrible."

"Yes, it is," the pastor responded. "Anyway, a member of our church has offered to take the children in until things can be sorted out. He knows the way to the airport. However, the children do not really know him. They have stayed with him in the past, and their parents were close to them before they went to Australia. I know they know you well from Australia. I would like to make them feel as comfortable as possible due to the circumstances. Is there any way I can get you to stop by his house and ride down with him? He said if you were in the vicinity to stop by and get some supper as well. Then you guys could go get the children." Bro. Nickels stopped talking and gave Dylan a few minutes to absorb what he had just been told.

Dylan felt as if his life was happening in a bubble. He felt detached. He shook his head to try to clear it and then answered Bro. Nickels. "Yeah, I guess I can do that. How do I get to this house?"

After a few moments of directions, Dylan sat his cell phone back into the cup holder in the dash of his truck. What was going on? His whole life decided to collapse all at one time. He had been helping Bro. Genkins get a vehicle he could use in Australia to haul some people to his church. During that time, he had become very close to him. Seems to Dylan everything was going wrong at once. That old saying his mom used to tell him was making more and more sense by the moment: "When it rains, it pours."

He followed the directions Bro. Nickels had given him and pulled into the driveway at a quaint little house with wooden siding about five minutes later. He shut off the engine and clambered out of his truck. He still felt slightly dazed. What was the name of the person he was supposed to be seeing? Oh no. He had completely forgotten. He walked up to the door, noticing big, beautiful, purple pansies blooming at the side of the house. He paused and stared at them for a moment. This was the wrong time of the year for budding flowers. Someone loved flowers. He smiled. That reminded him of his grandmother. She planted flowers in the fall. She said no matter when they were planted, God's creations were always beautiful anytime of the year. She had proven that correct through years of planting flowers at all seasons of the year. He walked up the steps and knocked on the door.

Kristina opened the door, expecting to see her grandparents on the other side. What she saw shocked her. A tall, dark, black-haired, brown-eyed stranger stood on their doorstep. He was wearing a dark-brown T-shirt and dress pants. *A rather odd combination*, she thought. She noticed he seemed tired. His eyes were rimmed in red, and he looked distressed and slightly dazed. She smiled. "Hi, my name is Kristina. How can I help you?" Maybe there was something they could do to end this man's obvious stress. Perhaps he was lost.

Dylan paused and stared at the woman who opened the door. Was that an Australian flag on this Kristina woman's necklace? No, it couldn't be. He shook his head. *Get a grip, dumbo. She is waiting on you to answer her.* He noticed her light-pink cardigan that offset her light-blue eyes and long straight blonde hair. He smiled at her. "Hi, I am Dylan McKendricks, and I am looking for a man who is supposed to be picking up Bro. Genkins' children at the airport," he said.

He immediately saw a difference in her. Her eyes filled with tears, and she chokingly told him to come in. He stared at her. What had he said? He didn't remember saying anything to offend anyone.

Kristina looked at the man and tried to contain the stab of pain she felt when he said the name Bro. Genkins. It was no use. She felt the pain welling up in her heart about the same time tears started streaming down her face. She looked at Dylan and tried to smile. But it was of no use. She looked over at her dad, who nodded.

She stepped around him, walked out the door, and back into the breezy summer air. Oh, but it hurt deep inside. She felt like her heart was going to break in half. The people of Australia needed a missionary—more than one missionary. They needed many missionaries to help them. They needed missionaries to lead them to Jesus. As she walked, she noticed a dark-brown truck sitting in the driveway. *It must belong to Mr. McKendricks*, she thought. She walked on by the truck and then stopped, turned around, and walked back to the front of the truck. There lying on the ground in front of his truck was a colorful piece of paper. As she walked up to it, she stooped down and picked it up. On the front in blaring red letters were the words "Have a burden for the people of Australia?"

She felt the blaring shock gently easing the pain in her heart as she devoured every word on that piece of paper. "Have a burden for the people of Australia? Please pray for Bro. Dylan McKendricks as he strives to take the gospel to this needy nation." There, off to the side, was a picture of a smiling, happy version of the man who was standing in her house right at that moment. She felt a warm feeling gradually sweep through her. He was a missionary. Not just any missionary, but a missionary to Australia.

She started crying again. Her mind was whirling. *Here he is. The missionary I need to be praying for next. The next person to fill my everyday prayer life like Brother Ryan and Mrs. Carrie did. This is so wonderful. I have to go back inside and meet this man.*

She ran into the house and slammed the door behind her in her haste. Everyone at the table looked up at her as she ran into the room. Her eyes were wet with tears. Tear tracks ran down her face. Her hair was windblown, and her nose was red and sniffling. She only had eyes for one person. She stared at Dylan until he started to get skittish.

Dylan stepped into the house feeling terrible. What had he said to offend the girl? He looked at the man at the table and spoke up. "I am so sorry. I have no idea what I did to offend her," he said, feeling worse by the minute. *Dylan, you jerk. She was so nice to you, and just because you are upset that your world is turning upside down, and you cannot have a wife even though you want one gives you no excuse to take it out on a poor innocent girl.*

A tall blond-headed man at the table smiled. Dylan looked carefully over at him and noticed it was the same man who had nodded at the girl and gave her the permission to run off like that. The man spoke up. "Hi, I am David Jason, and don't worry about that she will be fine. She was really close to Bro. Genkins and his wife. The news of them passing on has been hard on her. You must be the missionary Bro. Nickels told me to be expecting. Please have a seat," he said, smiling all the while.

Dylan felt even more dazed. "What, the girl is upset because Brother Ryan and Mrs. Cassie passed away?" He asked. He must have been hearing wrong. Besides, he had a reason to feel dazed, that stew sure smelled good.

"Yes, she thought a lot of them," David responded.

Dylan took the proffered seat and smiled at all the people surrounding the table. There was a tall gray-headed man with kind blue eyes, a slightly plump older lady with gray hair and green eyes, and three young boys ranging in size and age, all with blond hair and blue eyes. There was a young boy about eleven with brown hair and brown eyes and a lady with a kind face who had brown hair and sparkling green eyes. She reminded him of the girl who had answered the door.

That must be her mom, he mused. And the last person sitting at the table was Bro. David Jason. *This must be his family*. He put everything together in his mind. It was Bro. Jason's sons, his wife, and either his parents or her parents. He continued to smile rather stupidly as he scanned the family once more, then he looked over at the man of the house. "You have a nice-looking family," he complimented, taking heed to what his dad had told him once before when he was younger.

"Son," he had said. "When you are invited to another man's home, be grateful for what he gives you, and be grateful if you are surrounded by a family who looks as though they are all loved. When you are in that atmosphere, that man deserves your praise. Be sure to tell him you think he has a nice family. It might make a difference." Dylan smiled fondly at the memory.

"Why, thank you, young man," Bro. Jason replied. "Here, I will introduce them to you." He smiled at Dylan and pointed to the door. "The girl who answered the door and led you to believe you had said something offensive was my Australia-crazed daughter, Kristina."

Dylan jerked. *Did he say Australia-crazed? No. Dylan, you really need to get a grip now. You are hearing ridiculous things.* "That's a unique name." Dylan listened to him, all the while telling himself to grow up and quit forcing himself to believe he was hearing things he wasn't really hearing. For crying out loud, that made the second thing the man had said that he had heard incorrectly. *Get a grip, Dylan.*

"This is my beautiful wife, Melony," Bro. Jason said interrupting Dylan's thoughts as the kind-looking lady smiled and waved at him.

"Hi," she said.

"Hi," he answered, a dazed look crossing his face. He had to find out what that man had really said. This was driving him insane. "I'm sorry, sir," he spoke up. "But just a minute ago, did you say 'Australia-crazed'?" He felt slightly silly for asking such a stupid question when he knew he had heard incorrectly. *That man is going to think I'm nuts.*

"Yes," Bro. Jason laughed. "I did say she was Australia-crazed. She has a burden for that country so much that sometimes it is unbelievable. We were actually trying to plan a trip up there for her to visit Bro. Ryan and Mrs. Cassie. Her dream and heart-felt desire has always been to go to Australia and work with those native people. That's almost all of her problem with the Genkins's death. She feels there are too few missionaries in Australia as it is. Now there are even less, and it really bothers her." He finished.

David smiled at the young man that was sitting at his table. When Bro. Nickels had told him about this young man, he had mentioned he was single and had been looking for a wife. He hadn't said anything to Melony about it, just in case his hunch was wrong. But it didn't seem to be. The young man had checked out to be a missionary, and he seemed to be interested in the fact Kristina was Australia-crazy. David had a gut feeling this would not be the last time by a long shot this young man ate at his table.

Dylan felt shock ripple through him. Wait…was what the man said for real? The woman had a burden for the people of Australia. Oh, well this was good. Maybe she could be of some assistance helping him pray for the recently widowed Carolyn and her now fatherless children as they struggled with Matt's death. He smiled at David briefly. "Oh. Okay, sorry. I thought I had misunderstood what you said."

"No, it's quite all right. These young men are my sons. This is David," He said returning back to the introductions, pointing to the brown-haired boy who smiled and nodded at Dylan. "Seth," he motioned to the oldest blond-haired boy who smiled at him. "Jon," he gestured over to the blond boy seated in the middle of the bench. Dylan thought he was probably the middle son, but he wasn't going to speak up and ask he had already made enough blundering errors.

David continued with his introductions oblivious to the direction Dylan's thoughts had taken. "And this last blond on the end is my second oldest son, Abel," David finished, looking over at Dylan. "These very nice-looking older people on the end of the table are my in-laws, my wife's parents. Jonathon and Chelsea." David took a seat, smiling at Dylan.

Dylan felt slightly dazed for the second time in a matter of minutes. That was a lot of people to try to remember. He smiled at everyone and said to David, "Thanks for introducing me." He noticed that across the table Mrs. Jason seemed to be getting agitated. She kicked her husband under the table and nodded toward him.

What could be wrong? Did I say something? he wondered, but his fears were laid to rest as David stood back up with a sheepish smile on his face. He turned to the people at the table and stepped out to the end embarrassment flushing his face a deep red. "Well, I introduced you guys to him, but I forgot to introduce him to you guys," he said.

Dylan smiled in amusement as he noticed everyone at the table was also getting amused at David's mistake.

"Everyone, this is Bro. Dylan McKendricks, missionary to Singlow, Australia." David said, his eyes twinkled with suppressed mirth.

Dylan smiled and waved. He immediately noticed Mrs. Jason watching him with an increased intensity. *I have got to have something wrong with me*, he thought, feeling ashamed but why he wasn't really sure. He watched as she slowly shook her head as if to clear her thoughts then nodded toward the stew and smiled.

"Have some stew, Bro. McKendricks," she said, passing him the ladle.

He sat down and took the ladle. He ladled some stew into his bowl just as David returned to his seat. He returned the ladle to the pot and took a spoonful of soup after saying a quick blessing. He didn't know why Mrs. Jason was staring at him. But it was starting to make him feel very uncomfortable, and strange. *I just know something is wrong with me or perhaps I have something on my clothing*.

Right at that moment the door burst open.

There stood Kristina. Her eyes were wet with tears. Tear tracks ran down her face. Her long blonde hair blowing with the wind caught his attention for a moment, and then he noticed her nose was red and she was sniffling.

He felt a pull toward her as he realized she was experiencing at least some of the same pain he was struggling with. He watched her search the room seemingly frantic with her eyes until they finally landed on him. Then she proceeded to stare at him until he started to get skittish. Now he knew he had to have something weird stuck on him somewhere. Why else would everyone be staring at him as if he were crazy? He looked down at his clothes, reached up, and felt his hair. Everything felt fine. He noticed his prayer card in her hand, glanced up at her face, and smiled as realization dawned on him. Her dad had said she was upset because there weren't many missionaries in Australia. That could be the reasoning behind her tears. *Maybe everything is okay. Maybe she is just shocked that I am a missionary to Australia. Her dad did not seem to have told any of the others I was coming. Maybe they are all shocked.* He grinned as he finally reached a reasonable solution as to why everyone would be staring at him. He could be a surprise to everyone. So it wasn't that anything was technically wrong with him, just that he was unexpected. Those types of things often made people act different than they normally would.

CHAPTER 12

Kristina stared unashamedly at the young man seated at the table. He had smiled at her in a friendly way. He also was a missionary to Australia. She felt like she was clutching at something that was not there. But the thoughts of there actually being more than the three missionaries she always prayed for every day that were going to Australia was overwhelming.

"Are you the missionary to Australia?" she asked, still staring at him rather rudely.

Dylan looked at Kristina, once again assessing what he saw. For some really odd reason, she was still staring at him, and it was beginning to annoy him once again. Why would anyone stare at another person in such a manner? It wasn't like he had something wrong with his clothing, he had already double and triple checked it. He was starting to feel very uncomfortable in this situation. He glanced over towards the door, and decided he would give them a little while longer to adjust to his presence before he left. Everyone in the room was looking at him, he noticed, looking around the room again.

"I hate to sound rude or mean," he stated, "but for crying out loud, why are all you people staring at me?" He sounded a lot gruffer than he originally meant to sound.

David grinned and then looked at him. "Well, son, we are not actually staring at you. We are watching you, waiting to see what your response to my rather eager daughter is going to be." David answered his question, amusement shimmering in his eyes.

Dylan looked at him in astonishment. Eager? She didn't seem eager to him. She seemed upset. And to be honest, she was starting to scaring him a little bit with all her constant staring.

"Yes, I am a missionary. A missionary to Singlow, Australia, to be exact," he responded, smiling coldly at her, slightly miffed she was continuing to stare at him. Not only was it making him uncomfortable. To just stare at anyone was also against any rules of etiquette his mom had ever taught him, particularly one that was a guest in your home. No matter how startled or curious you might be.

Kristina felt hot tears welling up in her eyes. She saw astonishment cross the young missionary's face as she started crying. "It is so nice to meet you," she said, her sudden, unexpected grin nearly splitting her face in half. She stuck her hand out in front of him expecting him to shake it. "I am Kristina."

Dylan shook her hand as he looked at this strange girl standing in front of him. "It's nice to meet you too," he replied. Smiling warmly in response as he realized that she was genuinely glad to see him. "My name is Dylan McKendricks. I hear you have a burden for the people of Australia, and I see you have our Australian flag on your necklace." He was still smiling at her.

My, what a wonderful smile, Kristina thought, noting how his even white teeth contrasted with his dark, summer tan. *He noticed my flag*, she thought with a grin briefly crossing her face. *My, he's handsome. Good grief. Kristina, get control of yourself. He is God's man. He's a missionary, not something for you to be analyzing.*

"Yes, I pray for the people of Australia as often as I can. Which I am afraid is not quite often enough. I wish there was something else I could do to help," she said remorsefully, tears shimmering in her eyes.

Dylan watched this beautiful girl in front of him. *You could marry me so I wouldn't have to be alone.* He gasped aloud at the direction his thoughts had taken. Where had that even came from? Hadn't he just got done trying to figure out why these strange people were staring at him?

"Is everything okay?" David asked, starting up out of his chair at Dylan's audible gasp.

"Aah, y-yes, s-sir," Dylan said with a slight stammer. "Everything is fine." He smiled at David, trying to relieve his fears. *Dylan, get a grip of yourself, man. She is a woman. She is a person, a human being, not someone for you to be dictating what she does. Besides, a girl like her would never marry someone like you*, he thought. "I'm sure you can find something else you can do," he said turning to face Kristina. "It might take some time. But God will let you know what his plan is for you and your life."

Kristina watched as he gasped and wondered briefly what he had been thinking. He had looked awfully funny when her dad asked if he was okay. He had started as if he had something to hide. He was also being very thoughtful, reassuring her God had a plan for her to follow. Goodness, but did she ever need to hear that. Recently, seeing that God had a plan for her life had been one of the biggest things she had been struggling with. He had no way of knowing that, and yet he had addressed it so easily. That appealed to her more than she cared to admit, even to herself. That meant he had a close walk with God.

She smiled at Dylan and spoke up sadness cloaking her voice. "I know he does have a plan for me, and I also know that he will show me his will, but for some reason, knowing it and truly believing it are totally different. And I am afraid I am having a hard time truly believing it right now."

Dylan started. Wow, this girl was sure full of completely random surprises. He had been discussing that exact same thing with James just a few short hours ago. Apparently, unlike what he had originally thought, he wasn't the only person who was facing that sad dilemma. "I know exactly what you mean," he stated briefly. "I have been struggling with the same things recently." His voice suddenly filled with pain. "I wish there was something I could say to help you with it, but unfortunately, as I am still in the same predicament, I can't say any words of encouragement that could possibly be of any assistance."

He smiled and looked over at David. "What time do we have to go pick up the children?" he asked, wanting to leave as this situation was getting a little bit uncomfortable.

Kristina watched as pain started shimmering in the missionary's eyes, and she was sorry she had caused him pain. Then it hit her exactly what had just transpired: he had said he had been going through the exact same thing recently. She was not in this thing alone no matter how she felt. She smiled as he became visibly unsettled and started wanting to leave. She turned and watched her dad get an amused expression on his face and knew that he had noticed Dylan's discomfort as well.

"Right now," David answered, glancing up at the clock to check the time and then grinning softly over at his daughter. He reached over and kissed his wife then walked to the door and grabbed his jacket in case it turned off cold like the weatherman had called for.

Dylan followed right behind him, feeling more and more unsettled. *Something about these people is unsettling*, he thought. Not feeling very hospitable, but being true to himself he smiled, then he grabbed his jacket from where he had laid it having heard the weather on the way over and stepped out the door behind David.

CHAPTER 13

Dylan followed along behind David to a nice van parked near the curb. He glanced over it, noticing the side said Shining Light Baptist Church. Bro. Nickels pastored that church. He looked back over to David curious as to whether this was the vehicle they were taking. David was stepping into the driver's seat. Dylan followed suite and stepped up into the passenger seat and fastened his seat belt. He glanced over at David and smiled. "Did you borrow this van from your church?" he asked, rather curious if the man attended Bro. Nickels or if perhaps he got names mixed up.

"Yes, I did," David answered "This is the old van our church used to use awhile back. I don't have a vehicle large enough to carry my family plus all four of the Genkins children. So Bro. Nickels said I could borrow the old church van to save us some gas. Without it in order to carry all of us, we would have had to drive all three of our vehicles which of course would have ran our gas bill way up." David turned onto the main highway the van growing quiet as both men sank into thought.

As they headed down the interstate, Dylan's thoughts returned to a few moments before when he had been in the house with that man and his family. What in the world had he been thinking? What had caused his thoughts to go toward marriage? He did not even know the girl. He shook his head. *I am acting crazy.*

David drove down the road thinking about all that had gone on that day. Everything was quickly changing in his life, and in the lives of the people surrounding him. In just the past few minutes since Bro. McKendricks had shown up at his home, the thought of the possibility of the young man and Kristina getting married had crossed his mind several times. Bro. Nickels had told him that Dylan had been struggling with being alone especially in Australia for quite some time. Apparently, being alone in Australia was not very appealing to a young man. Bro. Nickels had told him that he thought God might have brought Dylan here to meet Kristina, and David wasn't one hundred percent sure he didn't have something there. The only thing about the idea of them getting married that really bothered him was that Dylan would be heading back to Australia in a matter of only a couple of days. And once he got back because of his visa, it would be a while before he came back to the United States again. Therefore, that meant one of two things. Either they would have to get married in a matter of days, or she would have to wait on him to return. David sighed. Neither one of those ideas were very appealing to him. The thought of his daughter being a missionary wife wasn't as scary as it one time had been.

However, the thought of her being in Australia with a man he barely knew did scare him. Surely, God wouldn't ask that of him right. Oh, who was he kidding? Somehow, he knew Kristina would be leaving soon. And although he loved her, he would not stand in the way of God's will. Even if Dylan wasn't God's will, with her burden for the people of Australia, it wouldn't be long before God made it clear what he wanted her to be doing. David smiled and glanced over at Dylan. "So, how well do you know the children?" he asked.

Dylan looked at David startled out of his thoughts. It was obvious he had been lost in thought. "I know them pretty well. I spent quite a bit of time with their father some time ago. We helped each other out as much as possible. There aren't many of us out there so we rely on each other."

"Okay, that's good. Maybe you being here will help them feel more at home," David said, pulling into the airport.

"Yeah, I think that was what Bro. Nickels was thinking when he invited me to come along and help you pick them up," Dylan replied. Then he softly grinned. "Besides, it gives me a chance to get to talk to you a little bit, not much, grant you, but a little bit."

"Yeah, it will still be a few minutes before the plane gets here, but I could tell you needed to get out of that house," David said, turning off the engine and shifting to look Dylan in the face.

Dylan smiled as he felt the heat mounting in his face turning him a brilliant shade of red. "I'm sorry about that. I'm afraid I am a little bit touchy about that subject. I am having a rough time truly trusting that God has a plan, and in his own time, He will show it to me, and talking with your daughter made that pain fresh in my mind." Dylan said, feeling rather sheepish.

"I understand," David said, "I have struggled with waiting on God before in the past, but you just have to trust. I know it's hard now, but it's better than messing up your whole life by jumping ahead of God's will." He noticed Dylan's sheepish look and quickly addressed it. "It's nothing to be embarrassed about. It's something every person faces at some point in their life." David smiled. "And besides, God's will for your life might not be as faraway as you think."

"I hope so," Dylan said. "I don't mean to sound bad, but I am tired of waiting. I am so tired of being alone, going home at night to be by myself. I literally come home to a house resounding with emptiness. There is no supper, no wife to hug, not a living thing. It is just furniture and open space. I feel so lonely. I know God is there always, but it's not the same as having a person there you can converse with. I also know you can talk to God about everything, but again it's still not the same." Dylan hoped he didn't sound like he was putting down his faith in God. He wasn't. He was only trying to explain his feelings on the matter.

"I know it's not the same," David said sympathetically. "Don't lose heart. You still have a few days before you go back. Who knows what might happen during that period of time. God can work miracles like he did in the bible times you know."

"I know, but I don't even know any girls that I could possibly consider marrying," Dylan said.

"Well. I am not sure if you meant that literally, but my daughter is single," David responded.

"Oh, really? Well, okay then, I know one girl I could consider," Dylan replied, smiling.

"I am not trying to sound like an old-fashioned person, but how many girls do you honestly need to have the possibility of marrying?" David asked.

"Well, ah, just one," Dylan replied, grinning. "But I don't know. I mean, I don't know your daughter, and besides, I don't have your permission to court her. In addition, I don't know if it's God's will for us to be together. She might find me repulsive for all I know." *Are we really having this discussion? And did I honestly just say that out loud?* he wondered, grimacing. *Nice going, Dylan. She is attracted to me, she has a burden for Australia, she wants to go to Australia, and the next thing I know, I am actually considering courting a girl I have never even held a real conversation with based on these facts. This is nuts.*

David noticed the tone of Dylan's voice. The young man was really discouraged. And he didn't have the means to pick him up out of the dumps. Only God held that power. *God, what should I do?* he prayed silently. *Should I give him permission to court Kristina?* Personally, he didn't want to give Dylan permission, but he felt like God was nudging him in that direction. *Oh God, please give me the courage to do what you want me to do*, he prayed silently.

"Dylan, I want to tell you something. I need to pray about it, but I will pray about whether or not it's God's will for you two to court. I want you to think about it and pray about it. You let me know what conclusion you come to, and we will talk about it. Okay, son?" David asked, feeling slightly scared. Grown men were not supposed to feel this scared. He so did not want to give up his daughter. But if that was what God wants, then he would be better off allowing his daughter to stay in God's will than to keep her out of God's will. He knew, without a shadow of a doubt, whatever he told Kristina, she would follow. Even if she thought his decision was the wrong one, she would abide by it. She always had.

Dylan started. *What? He would honestly think about it? That's a nice thought.* He turned to David and smiled. "I will pray about it, and thank you," Dylan said, tears shimmering in his eyes.

"It's okay. Who am I kidding? I want my daughter to be in God's will. You could very well be it," David responded, smiling. "Come on, it's time to go get the children." David smiled.

"Okay," Dylan answered, climbing down out of the church van.

CHAPTER 14

Kristina caught her breath. He was so handsome. She didn't remember ever seeing a man that was that handsome before. What was wrong with her? She had never thought about a man like this before. Most men she knew in her opinion were not even close to being handsome, so she had never really contemplated the fact that there was a man somewhere that she would find really handsome. He was a missionary to Australia. That thought really intrigued her.

Maybe he is the one. The thought that crossed her mind randomly stopped her in her tracks. She paused walking up the stairs and assessed what she had just been thinking. Where had that came from? What had just happened?

I think he is handsome. And the next thing I know, my thoughts are turning toward marriage? That's crazy. Kristina, get a grip. Those things only happen in the movies, she tried to convince herself. Besides marriage was a huge step. One she wasn't sure she was ready to take yet. Even though she had wanted a husband for years. That was a step that would change the rest of her life. She would never be the same girl once she said "I do".

Several minutes after climbing out of the van, Dylan climbed back in. It hadn't taken long to pick the children up. He smiled, listening to the chatter of Bro. Genkins' children in the background as they discussed staying with Kristina and the Jason's; apparently, from the looks of things, it had not really hit them yet that their parents were dead. He would sure hate to be there when they did realize it. Since it was going to still be some time before church, when they got back, he decided he would go check in at the hotel and stay there for a little while. Maybe pray about this situation that had suddenly arisen with him and the Jason girl. Who would have thought that he would even be considering marriage with someone he didn't even know? Certainly not him. Marriage wasn't something to be entered into lightly. And even though he wanted a wife, he wasn't sure if entering into a marriage so suddenly would be the correct option. All the things it would change, the people that would be effected by such a marriage overwhelmed him.

David couldn't believe he had told Dylan to pray about marrying Kristina. He after all was her father, he was supposed to be providing for her. Making sure she didn't make wrong decisions if he could prevent it, and he had just encouraged a young man he didn't even know to consider marrying his daughter. Marriage was hard. It was different and it took a special kind of person to withstand all the trials it added to lives. Why would he deliberately make it harder on her, by encouraging her to marry someone she didn't know. What with all the normal nervousness, and trials of a new marriage, entering into such a thing with someone you barely even knew was bound to make her life miserable. *What is the matter with me?* he wondered. Goodness. He was going to have to tell Melony. That thought scared him. She would accept it. She was very submissive, but it would be hard for her to face the possibility of such a thing taking place. Sure, she would be excited that there was a possibility of Kristina getting married. But once the reality hit her, she would be very upset. *Look at me, thinking about it as if it was a certain thing.* He admonished himself. Son, I know the plans I have for you, thoughts of good and not of evil to give you an expected end.

David paused and reflected on what he had just heard. It hadn't been audible, but as sure as he was breathing. God had spoken to his heart. Now all he had to do was follow.

Almost thirty minutes later, Dylan pulled into the hotel planning to rest and think over the startling things that had happened in the past few hours. Once they had gotten back to the Jason's house, he had not even gone inside. If the children had been visibly upset, he would have gone inside and tried to help comfort them to the best of his ability, but since they were seemingly okay, he went ahead and left. He had a lot to think about now that he had spoken with Bro. Jason. Even after praying, he wasn't sure he had expected God to actually send him a wife before he left. It was one of those times when you prayed because you want it to happen, but you don't really expect it to happen and it still might not happen, but Dylan had a funny feeling that this was it. He had found the one. He didn't want to be one of these people who accepted the first person who came along and was available, but God had had a reason for sending him here. And he would like to believe this was it.

But let's face the reality, Dylan. The likelihood of this actually happening is slim to none, he tried to convince himself. But the truth of the matter was it was very possible. It could really finally be happening. He felt slightly excited at the thought that it could happen. He might not be going back to Australia alone. Although the thought was exciting, it was also scary. Marriage was a very important step. One that would require his complete dedication. Even if he didn't always feel like giving it.

He walked into the hotel and asked for his room thoughts still whirling around in his mind. A few moments later, he walked into room 207. It was a rather large room with a single king-size bed. It was beautiful on the inside. Green and brown curtains hung on the windows with black drapes behind them you could pull into place to block out the light and prying eyes if needed. A solid-brown comforter was on the bed, and three huge fluffy pillows were lying at the head of the bed. A nightstand containing a large lamp stood on the right side of the bed alongside a cabinet to put things in.

He put his suitcase in the cubbyhole that was to his right as he walked in the door. He opened his laundry bag, got out his clothes to wear to the camp meeting that night, grabbed his Bible, and went and carefully kneeled at the bedside. He checked his clock to make sure of the time; six forty-seven p.m., it read. That meant he had about forty minutes as Bro. Nickels meeting started at seven thirty p.m. It was about a five-minute drive from where he was staying, and he wanted to be a few minutes early if at all possible. He laid his Bible on the foot of the bed and took a deep breath forcing his mind to focus. *So many things I need to pray about*, he thought.

He closed his eyes and folded his arms on the bed, putting his head on his folded arms. "Dear Heavenly Father, there are so many things I need to pray about. But first and foremost on my mind right now is Kristina. God, I have been praying for a wife for a long time, and I know in your own time you will send me the perfect mate. God, I want to believe Kristina is the one, but only you know for sure. Please show me your will for my life in this situation. Please grant me the grace to accept your answer and the courage to act upon it. I don't want to do the wrong thing. I know that marrying the wrong woman could cost me my ministry and my life as I know it. Marriage in and of itself is a huge step to take, and it scares me Lord. Please help me to know what to do."

Dylan continued to pray, pouring his heart out to the Lord. "I want to believe this is what you want me to do. Can you please help me not to act on my feelings but to act on what I know to be your will in this situation? And, God, please help me as I go back to Australia. Please keep me safe. Thank you for helping the Genkins children with this transition. Please help them to go on once the news of their parents' death does become real to them. Thank you for helping them arrive safely and for keeping David and I safe as we went and picked them up from the airport. Once again, thank you for helping me to get tickets going back to Australia at a reasonable rate. Please help the Cartin family as they deal with her husband and their father, death. Please help me to deal with Matt's death. Sometimes the pain is so quick and sharp, it takes my breath away. I don't really understand it, but you do. Thank you for all you've done and all you are going to do. In Jesus' name, amen." Dylan closed out his prayer and kept his eyes closed resting for a few slight moments. He was so tired. That little nap at Bro. Candsly's had already worn off. He wondered when he would know for sure about Kristina and what God's will was concerning her. *Be patient, Dylan. He will answer you in his own time. Not your time. His time.*

CHAPTER 15

D ylan opened his eyes and glanced at the clock. It was seven fifteen p.m. *Oh, wow. I am going to be late*, he thought, rushing to his feet. He grabbed his clothes and ran to the bathroom. He quickly changed what he was wearing and, on his way out the door, grabbed his Bible and flipped off the light switch. He made his way to his truck and climbed in, the thoughts of the last day overwhelming him.

Had it really only been this morning when he had gotten the phone call that Matt had been killed? It seemed like days ago, he thought, headed down the highway. He checked his map to make sure of where he was going and smiled to himself. Trust him to think he was going to have a day off only at the close of the day for him to realize it was busier than one of his busy days. So much had happened in such a short span of time.

A few moments later, he pulled into the church parking lot and found a parking space. He noticed a white van beside the church that looked a lot like his parents' van. A pang on longing to see his family washed over him. He wished his parents could be there, but they had said there was no way they could afford to come, and as he was already short of funds, there was no way possible he could afford to pay for them to come. Sadly, even though he was only a few short hours away, he wouldn't get to see his family this time in. Since he was leaving so soon, all of those plans were canceled too. All of a sudden, he found it hard to breath as pain shot through him. He loved his family so much, and it had been almost three years since he had gotten to see and spend time with them. He missed them more than words could ever express. He wondered if anyone could ever get used to not seeing their family and then decided that they could not. It might become the normal thing not to see them for long periods of time, but you would always miss them, no matter what happened. He glanced over and saw the men from the church praying out in a large meadow a little ways off from the church building and briefly thought about joining them. After glancing at his watch, he decided he would just go on in the church. It would only be a few moments before they were done praying anyway, he reasoned. He noticed the van the Jason's had borrowed nearby where he had parked and noticed there was a young lady standing by the door. He watched as another young lady joined her, and it only took him a minute to recognize Kristina. Who was that with her? Her beautiful hair, and the form of her body made him think of Megan. Could it be his sister?

Wait! It can't be Megan. They can't come. For crying out loud, Dylan, get a grip of yourself. So much had happened in so short a time, that he was imagining things. He took another look finding that she still closely resembled his sister. He had to find out who it was. He started walking toward her just as she looked up.

"Dylan!" she screeched rather loudly. Her voice echoing across the land. Her face lit up with happiness, and her eyes glimmered with suppressed joy. She ran to him and put her arms around him. He laughed and spun her around until they were both breathless.

"Megan! What are you doing here?" he asked, a grin on his face.

"Well, Bro. Nickels raised up the money in an offering so we could come," she said, then smiling up at him, happiness glowing in her face. "Oh, Dylan. I missed you so much." Her eyes filled with tears of joy. The years of separation could never diminish all that they had shared together as brother and sister. The family memories, the closeness shared between them, could never be severed.

He smiled and hugged her tight. "I missed you too, lil' sis," he said, grinning and forcing back his own tears. His heart was a mixture of extreme happiness and sadness, that even though it had just began, it would soon be over. He pulled away from her and asked, "Where's everyone else?"

"Inside," she answered, not taking her eyes off him.

He turned and started walking toward the church as he noticed Kristina walking up beside him and Megan. He smiled over at her and continued walking. He was hoping that by the time they reached the church, that service wouldn't have started yet and he would have a few moments to talk to his parents. She looked beautiful in a flowing black skirt, a white blouse, and a navy blue jacket. Her long wavy blonde hair was pulled back in a clip, and she was wearing flat black shoes.

Wow, she's pretty, he thought, turning his attention back to where he was walking.

"Dylan," Megan said from his side, "have you met Kristina?"

He nodded and smiled. "Yes, I have," he responded, looking at his sister. "We met just a few hours ago at her house."

"At her house?" she asked, curiosity shining on her face.

"Yes, at her house. It's a rather long story," he said,

"Oh, that's neat. She is my best friend," Megan said, grabbing hold of his arm. "She loves Australia. You two should really talk."

Dylan blushed, the red slowly heating up his face, as he looked over at Kristina and noticed she was blushing as well. She poked Megan in the arm with her elbow. "Megan, don't say things like that," she admonished, her embarrassment apparent on her face.

"Well, personally, I don't think that's such a bad idea," he said, immediately noting Kristina's reaction.

Kristina started. What in the world was wrong with this man? First, she learns he is her best friend's brother, then he weirdly encourages his sister to set them up. *Does he have a problem with his head?* she wondered. Gosh, but that blue shirt set off his dark brown eyes and black hair. He was so handsome. *Kristina. Stop it*, she commanded herself. Since when was a guy's handsomeness a good sign of his character?

Never. So she needed to stop paying attention to those things and wonder about his character.

"Okay, so, Megan, how long do you guys get to stay?" she asked breathlessly.

"We are staying for the whole meeting," Megan replied, grinning wickedly at Kristina. "Handsome, isn't he?" she whispered to Kristina, her eyes dancing with merriment.

Oh no, she did not. She didn't just say that where he could hear, Kristina tried to convince herself, glancing over at Dylan. He smiled at her knowingly. His eyes were dancing.

"Well, am I?" he asked, his eyes filled with laughter.

"Oh, Dylan," Megan said, acting as if she was embarrassed he had caught her asking Kristina such a question. "Don't make a big fuss out of it."

"Oh, I'm not making a big fuss out of it. I am just curious as to what Ms. Jason is going to say," he replied, laughing slightly.

Kristina gasped. *Oh my gosh! He heard that.* She felt like her face was on fire. She didn't think she had ever been that embarrassed. What was she going to tell him? That she thought he was handsome? *No way. Then he would think I was throwing myself at him*, she admonished.

"Well?" he questioned Kristina, still grinning.

Kristina smiled back. "I guess you would do in a pinch," she responded merrily.

Megan laughed, and Dylan grinned sheepishly. "I guess I deserved that," he said, smiling and noting how flushed Kristina had become.

"You guess?" Megan needled him.

"Okay. I deserved that," he said as they walked into the vestibule of the church. He noticed his mother standing off to the side and practically ran to give her a hug and say hello. "Mom! I have missed you so much," he said, throwing his arms around her.

She smiled, tears shimmering in her eyes. "I've missed you too, son," she said, hugging him back, squeezing him so hard he felt like he was going to pop.

He gently pulled away and smiled. She returned his smile then motioned behind him. "Come on over here, sweetheart. I want to introduce you to someone," she said, speaking to someone behind him. He turned to find none other than the beautiful Ms. Kristina Jason standing there.

She glanced at him and flushed a scarlet red. *He knows. He knows I truly think he's gorgeous,* she thought, trying to smile. "We've already met," Kristina said.

"Yes, I can see that now," Sarah said, smiling as she noticed the way her son watched Kristina and the way Kristina had flushed a knowing light entering her eyes. "Well, Dylan. This young lady is like a member of our family. She came up last year and spent all summer with us to help us prepare for our fall camp," she said.

Dylan started. *This young lady is like a member of our family. She is my best friend. My Australia-crazed daughter. She is so upset about Bro. Ryan's and Mrs. Cassie's death. She is more upset about the fact there is no one there to preach to the Australians than the fact they are actually gone. My daughter is single. Dylan, I want to tell you something. I need to pray about it, but I will pray about whether or not it is God's will for you two to court.*

Statements he had heard in connection to Kristina in the past few hours flooded his mind just as the knowledge hit him without a shadow of a doubt she was the one. She was the one God wanted him to marry. The knowledge both excited and frightened him. This would be a huge step and one he wouldn't recommend to anyone else. He briefly closed his eyes. *Thank you, Lord, for sending her to me, and thank you for giving me an answer so quickly. Now, would you please help me to act upon it?* he prayed.

"Um, Dylan?" Sarah asked, her eyes filled with concern.

He startled in surprise and glanced up. All at once, he remembered that she had been talking to him. "Oh, sorry, Mom. I had something on my mind. That's wonderful," he said, a sheepish look crossing his face. "So, you like helping people prepare for things?" he asked, addressing Kristina with a smile.

She looked up, startled. He was talking to her, and as she returned his smile, a flush quickly rose in her cheeks once again. *Kristina, for crying out loud, he's a missionary, not a possible suitor. Quit getting embarrassed when he speaks to you.* "Yes, I like helping anyone do anything I possibly can," she replied, smiling.

He grinned. "That's good. Helping people do things that need to be done is always a good thing. Good people deserve good help," he said, feeling rather silly. *That was a stupid thing to say. Helping people do things is always a good thing. Duh. Man, get a grip.*

"Um…yes, it is. And yes, they do," she replied, smiling.

He noticed her eyes held quite a bit of amusement and mentally kicked himself. What a stupid thing to say. "I guess I had better find a seat," he said as he noticed the men that had previously been outside praying started filing in and several more families had come in.

"Okay, Dylan," Sarah said, smiling, a knowing look in her eye and amusement on her face.

He scowled at her. He was not trying to be disrespectful, but that look she was giving him was annoying. He knew what he had said was slightly ridiculous, but she did not have to rub it in. She grinned and winked at him, taking her seat.

"It was nice talking to you, Bro. McKendricks," Kristina said, smiling and walking off.

"You too, Ms. Jason," he responded, walking in the opposite direction before he said anything else he would later live to regret. What had possessed him to say such a silly thing?

CHAPTER 16

After Dylan walked off, Megan grabbed Kristina's arm. Her eyes were sparkling with laughter. "'He'll do in a pinch,'" she mocked, giggling. "You think he's handsome!" She giggled harder.

"Okay. I think he's handsome, gorgeous in fact. What's the difference?" Kristina said, smiling at Megan's enthusiasm. *Did I just tell his sister that I think he's gorgeous? Well, I don't know if having my best friend as a handsome man's sister is a good thing,* she pondered.

"Oh, really? It makes no difference. You love Australia and want to go there and help lead people to the Lord. He is a missionary to Australia. You are single and getting discouraged waiting on God to send you a husband. Dylan is sick of being alone in Australia and is practically begging God for a wife. He has been for a couple of years now. He was miraculously given tickets to come to the United States, and if I just heard him correctly when he was talking to Jim on the phone, then because of a tragic accident, this is the only place he is going to get to come to before he has to head back. Um, why do you think he's here?" Megan finished up, grinning as the implication she was making hit Kristina.

Wait, what? Is it possible? Could it really be true? God, could he be the one? No way, Kristina, that's too much of a coincidence, she tried to convince herself. She flushed and looked up at Megan. "I don't know why he's here. I guess because God told him to come," she answered, smiling. *Oh God. Could it be true? Is it possible he could be the one you have planned for me? God, is he the one?* She prayed, feeling sheepish. She was supposed to wait on God to bring her a man, not just assume the first man she met that could even possibly be the one was the man God intended for her.

Dylan took a seat beside his brother and grimaced. What was the matter with him? *God, thank you so much. Please help me. Please help the service tonight go according to your will.* He prayed as Bro. Nickels mounted the pulpit and started making announcements.

After service that night and everyone else was in bed asleep, David looked over at Melony who was brushing her hair and sitting on the side of the bed. He eased down on the bed beside her and took the brush away from her. "Honey, there is something I need to talk to you about," he said, trying to smile but failing. This was too big of a decision to be made half-heartedly.

"What is it, sweetheart?" she asked, reaching up and taking his hand.

"I'll tell you the details later if you wish, but earlier when Dylan and I went to pick the children up, the subject of his much-unwanted singleness came up. After talking to him for a few minutes and praying, I felt led to tell him we would pray about the possibility of Kristina and him courting and getting married," he said, watching her carefully waiting to see what her reaction would be. He knew she would back his decision eventually but it might take lots of explaining.

She visibly started and then smiled. "I had wondered if he was the one. Somehow, when I saw him standing in our doorway earlier and then tonight at church, when I heard him sing, it just felt so right," she said.

"I had hoped you would have had some thoughts on the matter already," he said, smiling. "What do you think we should do?"

"Well, to be honest, the first thing I think we should do is pray," she said.

"I agree, but we also need to discuss some things," he said.

She smiled. "Yes, but I think we should pray first and then discuss what we prayed about, plus all the other things."

"Okay," he said, smiling and taking her hands and pulling her up off the bed.

"Do you think it's possible he could really be the one?" she asked breathlessly.

"I think it's highly possible, and to be honest, after praying about it earlier today, I think it's highly likely," he responded.

She stood up, and they knelt down beside the bed together with bowed heads and humble hearts. After a while in prayer, they stood up and hugged.

"He's the one," she said, her voice muffled by his shirt.

"Yes, he is," David replied, tears starting to stream down his face.

"Why, sweetheart, what's wrong? This is a joyous occasion," she said, tugging playfully at his sleeve.

"I know it's a happy occasion, marriage is such a huge step for anyone to take. I know God will provide, but first of all, I have to let my little girl go real soon," he said. "And second, there is only one of two things that could happen now, and I feel there is only one that is the correct answer." He tried to sound happy, but failed miserably.

"Oh? And what are they?" she asked, curious.

"Well, they can either get married tomorrow or the next morning, or they can wait a couple of years until he can come back to the United States. From my understanding, it would be close to three years before he could return because of his visa," he said.

Melony gasped. "Are you serious?" she asked, tears welling up in her eyes.

"Yes, I am. I think you know which one I think they should do," he said, tears choking his throat.

"Yes, I know. I don't think they need to wait three years either," she said, burying her face into his shirt.

He cuddled her to him. "I guess it's a good thing Bro. Nickels canceled services tomorrow morning in honor of the

Genkins's death," he said, pulling her closer. "We will need to talk to both Dylan and Kristina tomorrow."

"Yes. I agree," she said, trying to smile.

"Come on. Let's go to bed," he said, pulling her down onto the bed.

She lay down on the bed and cried. Her tears drenched her pillow. Letting go of Kristina was going to be hard. But it wouldn't be as hard on her, as it would be her daughter. The whole family would need strength.

CHAPTER 17

The next morning, Dylan awoke bright and early. The sunshine came through his window, warming the air around him and making for a beautiful day. He stumbled up out of bed and walked over to the window, looking out over the hotel grounds. The morning was so peaceful and beautiful. He glanced at his watch; he had guessed pretty accurately. It was seven twenty-eight a.m. He had figured it was about seven thirty a.m. The sun shone brightly over the bushes, the rays making patches of the grass look light and other patches look dark. The dew was still on the ground, and the suns rays made it glisten like diamonds. He smiled. He had always loved mornings. He could hear birds chirping outside the window. He could see a robin flying around her nest in a bush not far from the window, such a beautiful thing, a mother and her children. He sighed. Then he stretched right as his cell phone rang. Who was calling? He wondered, stepping over to his phone. He looked at the screen. Unidentified caller. *Well, that could be any number of people*, he thought, smiling to himself. "Hello," he said into the receiver.

"Hi, Dylan. This is David Jason. I hope I didn't wake you," came a man's voice over the line.

"No, I wasn't asleep I had actually just gotten up. What's wrong?" he asked, feeling slightly scared something had happened to one of the Genkins.

"Oh, nothing's wrong. Sorry, I did not mean to worry you, but I wanted to talk to you. How soon can you be over here?" David asked, sounding alert.

"Um, well. I haven't taken a shower, ate breakfast, or changed clothes yet, so probably an hour," Dylan said, wondering what in the world Bro. Jason would have to talk to him about. Granted, he had something to talk to Bro. Jason about, so it would work out well for both him and Bro. Jason.

"Well, change clothes and take a shower, but don't worry about breakfast. Melony is still cooking. She just told me to invite you to come on over. If you hurry, we will have time to talk before breakfast. I want to get this over with as soon as possible," David said.

"Um. Are you sure everything's okay?" Dylan asked. "Because it sure sounds like something's wrong."

"No, nothing's wrong. I just want to talk to you about something," he replied, and Dylan could hear a smile in his voice.

"Okay. Well. Since it's obviously important, I'll try to be there in about ten or fifteen minutes," he said.

"Okay, that will be fine. That will give us a few minutes to prepare before you arrive," David said. "I'll see you when you get here then, son."

"Okay, see you in a few minutes," Dylan responded, closing the phone and rushing to his suitcase. So much for enjoying a nice quiet morning resting in the hotel. *I wonder what David wants to talk to me about?* He grabbed a pair of jeans and a T-shirt. He started walking to the bathroom to take a shower, and then he remembered he had forgotten his socks yesterday. He smiled. He about did the same thing again today. He grabbed a pair of socks out of his suitcase and walked to the bathroom. It wouldn't take him long to take a shower and change, then he would head over to find out what was going on over at the Jason's.

David looked over at his wife. She was frying sausage, getting ready to make some gravy. The smell that was wafting up from the pot had his stomach growling. He couldn't wait for breakfast time. He walked up behind her and put his arms around her. "Honey, do you think you can take a break?" he asked her, kissing the top of her head gently.

"Yes. Are we going to go talk to Kristina?" she asked.

"Yes, at least to let her know some of what's going on so Dylan's presence won't overwhelm her," he responded. He took her hand as they walked up the stairs. They looked into each other's eyes, both thinking the same thing: *Please help us, Lord.*

David reached up and knocked on the door. Knowing Kristina, she probably wasn't even up yet. He smiled. It always made him happy when he realized how well he knew his family.

Knock, knock, came the sound of someone knocking on her door as Kristina pulled a brown T-shirt with dolphins on it over her head. She had awakened sometime ago and had been thinking about the situation with the people in Australia. She had spent quite some time praying and had just gotten up and changed clothes. She walked to the door and opened it. On the other side stood her parents, both with tears shimmering in their eyes. They were holding hands. Kristina groaned. They had something else terrible to tell her. She didn't think she could handle another item of bad news. She was still reeling from yesterday's tragic happening.

"Is everything okay?" she asked, opening the door so her parents could come in.

They walked over to her bed and looked into each other's eyes.

Oh no, she thought. *God, please help me*, was both her next thought and prayer.

"Well, yes, honey. Everything is fine, but you might want to sit down," her mom replied with a smile.

Kristina walked over to the bed and took a seat, dreading what her parents were going to tell her next. Whatever it was had them all torn up, and she did not like it, not one bit. Her gut instinct was telling her what her parents had to say was important to her and her future.

"Okay, what is it?" Kristina asked, bracing herself for the worst.

"Well, Kristina. A young man is on his way over here so we can discuss you and him possibly courting or even getting married," her father started the conversation off hesitantly.

Kristina started crying. What? Had her dad really just said that a young man was hoping to court her? That was amazingly awesome. And also very frightening. Marriage was not something to be entered into lightly. She felt hot tears running down her face. "Who?" was the only question she could muster enough energy to say. She was so excited and scared.

"Dylan McKendricks," was her father's firm response.

"Megan's brother?" she asked, astonishment in her voice. "Are you serious? Oh my gosh," she said, laughing and crying all at the same time. Out of all the people she had thought her dad might possibly have said, this was the last. Now not only was she scared because she could be getting married, but also because she barely knew the young man.

"No, not Megan's brother. This is the young missionary, the one that was here last night," David replied, smiling at his daughter through his tears. She was obviously very happy but hesitant to say anything in any direction.

"That's Megan's brother," Kristina confirmed, now grinning. "Oh, Mom. He wants to court me." *Someone wants to court me.* Happiness filled her to the core. She had waited for this moment for so long, and now all she could do was cry and laugh.

"That's Megan's brother?" Melony said, glancing at her husband, noticing some of the stress leaving his face as her fears started abating. Well, at least they knew where he came from; that would help the matter a lot. They knew without a shadow of a doubt he had been raised in church and knew right from wrong. They smiled at one another, and then Melony glanced down at her daughter, who was still crying. "Yes, honey. He is considering it," she responded, smiling.

"After a lot of prayer last night and this morning, your momma and I feel that God has given us the green light to give him permission to court you or to marry you. Whichever he feels is God's will," David said, looking at Melony for strength and then glancing down at his daughter.

"M-m-marry m-m-me?" Kristina stammered, not sure she had heard him correctly.

"Yes. Oh, I forgot, you do not know the whole situation. He has to go back to Australia tomorrow, and because of his visa, he can't come back to the United States for close to three years," David said.

Kristina gasped. Three years? Three years! Well, that only left one option in her mind. Marry him before he left. Before he left? Wait. Her dad said he was leaving tomorrow. Fear gripped her as she looked up at her parents. "Can I have a few minutes to pray?" she asked, tears standing in her eyes, her fear becoming evident. How could she possibly make such a big decision in less than twenty four hours. If she agreed to marry him, she would be leaving not only her family and friends, but her country. Fear gripped her heart, wrenching through her like a vice. To marry him, she would need to be positive he was the one.

"Yes, of course," her dad said, reaching down and giving her a hug and a kiss.

Her mom bent down and looked at her. "If you need to talk about anything, just ask, okay?" she told her, giving her a warm hug and a smile hoping to comfort her.

"Okay, Mom," Kristina managed to choke out.

Her parents turned and left the room, leaving her alone to her thoughts. She buried her face in her pillow and burst out in tears, partly from fear and partly from happiness. She hadn't even considered the fact she might be married in a matter of hours; that scared her to the core. People were supposed to court for at least a few months before they got married. Everyone knew marriage changed everything. And she had always thought, even if she were to get married, then it would be to someone close to home in case something happened. If she agreed to this, she would be going where there was no one she knew. Only herself and her husband.

She got down on her knees beside her bed and bowed her head. "Oh, God, I am so scared. Is this man your will? Am I really supposed to get married today? Oh, God! Please help me," she prayed, tears drenching her bed. Blinding fear gripped her heart. After a few moments, she heard a truck pull up in the driveway. She started crying harder. Then as she heard a knock sound on the front door, a peace unlike anything she had ever known came over her. She knew without a shadow of a doubt that Dylan McKendricks was the man she was supposed to marry, be that today or any other day. She smiled. God had a plan. All she had to do was wait. She was getting more and more excited by the moment. The fear was still there, but part of it had been replaced by a deep peace she couldn't explain.

She opened her door with the intentions of going down and talking to her mom. And then it dawned on her. That gorgeous man from yesterday was downstairs, possibly even wanting to marry her. She was wearing an old T-shirt, a flannel skirt, and she hadn't even brushed her hair. She quickly shut and locked the door and walked over to the closet. She dragged out a blue T-shirt with an Australian flag on the front. It was her favorite shirt. She also took out a new blue jean skirt her grandmother had sent her for Christmas. Oh yeah, her grandmother was supposed to be here by now. *I need to ask mom and dad if they know what has happened to them*, she thought. She quickly changed her clothes and brushed her hair. She ran her straightener through her hair quickly and sprayed some hairspray to hold it in place. Then she slipped on some socks and practically ran down the stairs. She had heard the door close some time ago, and she strongly suspected Dylan and her dad were outside. She was curious where her dad's parents were. They were supposed to have been here yesterday. If something had happened to them, she would be devastated.

As she stepped into the kitchen, she heard the low drone of her father's voice and her grandpa's voice. *Wait, that was Grandpa Jason's voice I heard*, she thought and stepped into the kitchen. Relief flooding through her. If she could hear her grandpa, then they must be okay.

"Hey, sweetheart," her dad said, glancing up and smiling when he saw her. "Look who finally decided to join us."

"I see," she said, running over and giving them both huge hugs. "It is so good to see you guys." She smiled. "I was actually coming downstairs to ask Mom if she knew where you guys were. I was starting to get worried something might have happened." She laughed.

"Well, we got caught in traffic until late last night, so we decided to stop and get a hotel room instead of coming in at such a late hour," her grandpa responded, smiling.

About that time, a knock sounded on the door. "I wonder who that could be," Melony said, a twinkle in her eye as she stepped over to open the door.

Kristina felt a dreadful anticipation. She was so excited and that dreadful fear was starting to blind her once more. She felt her dad's hand on her shoulder and looked up into his face.

"It'll all work out. I love you," he said, smiling at her reassuringly.

"What's going on?" she heard her grandpa ask as her mom opened the door, and there he stood, all six feet of him.

He was wearing a green T-shirt with the words "Give Me a Vision" printed on top of an Australian flag and a pair of loose-fitting denim pants. He had on a pair of dark-brown tennis shoes and held a brown leather jacket in his hand. She noticed his brown eyes flashing, and a teasing grin lit his face as he noticed her assessing him.

"I'll tell you later, but you're probably putting eyes on your future grandson unless something else unexpected happens," David said, standing to his feet.

Kristina felt a blush darken her cheeks, and she smiled at Dylan. He grinned in response. Her mom smiled as she noticed the exchange and went back to the stove. David grinned as well when he saw them smiling at each other, and as he noticed the teasing look on Dylan's face, a thought flitted through his mind. *I wonder what that's about?* He was sure whatever it was, it would be very interesting.

CHAPTER 18

Dylan looked at Kristina for a moment. She looked so beautiful. Her blonde hair was shimmering in the soft light, and her bright-blue eyes were glittering with fear and excitement. He understood that well, his heart was hammering out the same pattern. After getting peace from the LORD, the fear wasn't quite as bad as it had been, but it still ricocheted through his heart. She looked slightly nervous as well, but if that was what she truly felt he wasn't sure. *Thank you, God. You did not have to send me a beautiful woman, but you did. Can you please ease some of this fear, if this is your will? Thanks,* he silently prayed. "Hello, Bro. Jason. What's up?" he asked, turning to David as he stepped out from behind the table.

David walked over to the door. He shook Dylan's hand and smiled. "Let's go outside and talk," he said, as the implication of what was taking place started to hit Dylan.

Kristina looked at her mom and smiled. "I hope everything goes okay," she said anxiously.

"It will, sweetheart. Don't worry," her mom said, laughing.

"What's going on here?" her grandma asked, smiling knowingly.

"That young man is a missionary to Australia, and unless I miss my guess, all three of us feel he is God's will for Kristina. David is going to talk to him about his feelings toward the matter," Melony responded, turning the sausage.

"What's his name?" were the next words out of her grandpa.

"Dylan McKendricks," Kristina quickly replied nervously.

"I thought something like this might be going on," her grandma said. "David and I hadn't had peace about Kristina ever getting married until recently."

Kristina gasped. *Oh my goodness. That is scary*, she thought. *God was preparing me all this time to marry a missionary to Australia, thus the burden and the longing to help them.* She shuddered.

"How do you feel about this situation, Kristina?" her grandmother asked, smiling.

"I am nervous and slightly scared, but I am very excited, and I think this is what God wants," Kristina responded, glancing anxiously toward the door. *I wonder what they're saying? I wonder what Dylan thinks about me?*

"That's a good sign," her grandmother whispered. "Don't worry, God's got everything under control." She sounded reassuring.

Dylan walked out to the garage with David. *He is going to talk to me about Kristina. That's good. That means I will not have to*

bring the subject up. He smiled as David sat down and patted the seat on the bench beside him.

The morning air was crisp, and the smell of wet flowers was almost overwhelming. Dylan took a seat and glanced around, noticing the beauty of God's creation around them. The beautiful trees, the shining lake off in the distance, the birds calling back and forth to one another. The squirrels were just starting to romp in the soft grass under the trees. He turned to David. "So, what's on your mind?" he asked, somehow already knowing the answer.

"I think you know," David responded, smiling. "Melony and I prayed about it last night until we got peace, and we talked to Kristina about it this morning. As far as any of us are concerned, you are free to marry her. But it is a huge decision. Marriage is not something to be entered into lightly, without any thought, or concern. Even though we feel it is God's will, you need to be one hundred percent sure, you are marrying the correct one."

David watched a play of emotions cross Dylan's face, fear, excitement, and several others the last of which was both happiness and gratefulness.

Dylan was so happy. He had doubted God would ever show him his plan and had given up hope of ever finding a wife. He had been sure he would have to go back to Australia alone. Yet here God was being wonderful once more and giving him a wife to take home with him. He thought about the possibility of marriage and took in a deep breath as fear overwhelmed him. Marriage would forever more change his life. Peace slowly crept through his heart. He briefly thought about all the things that had happened recently. Well, out of all things that had happened, this was the most exciting. *I am getting married. Oh my gosh! I am getting married!* he thought, a wide grin crossing his face. He turned to his future father-in-law. "Bro. Jason," he started.

"Excuse me, son, but I think the term you are looking for is *Dad*," David interrupted, then smiled.

"Oh, sorry, sir," he said, grinning. "Dad, then with your permission, after a lot of prayer and thought, I would like to take your daughter home with me to Australia." He felt slightly bad about taking the man's daughter away from him.

"Well, I give you my blessing, son, but you need to talk to her about it, and make sure you are positive before you talk to her." David replied, tears welling up in his eyes. This was it; he was actually going to have to let his daughter go to further the work of God in Australia. Somehow, even through the mixed emotions of happiness and pain, he realized that of all the things that had surprised him about this situation and came out of nowhere, the fact that Kristina was going to marry a missionary to Australia wasn't a surprise. He had known in the depths of his heart one day, something of this nature would happen. There had been a reason God had given her that burden for Australia. Both of them were older and mature, they would make the right decisions. They both knew that marriage was a huge step, and would take that into account before getting married.

"I will, Dad. I promise. And with your permission, sir, I would like to do that now," he added, smiling just before he got really nervous. *What if she doesn't want to go?* he thought just as David spoke up.

"That's fine. Right now would actually be just fine," David replied. "As a matter of fact, I think right now would be wonderful because nobody is going to eat until we know what's going to happen between the two of you." He laughed. He noticed the tension on Dylan's face. "Don't worry, son. It'll all work out."

"What do I say? What if she doesn't like me? What if she doesn't want to marry me or go to Australia?" he said nervously.

David laughed. "She does, son. Trust me, she does," he said, smiling. David stood to his feet and placed his hand on Dylan's shoulder. "Well, son, I'm going inside to talk to Kristina. You want to come?"

Dylan grinned up at him and stood to his feet, gratefulness shining in his eyes. "Thank you so much, sir. I imagine giving up your daughter like this can't be easy," he said.

"It's not, but it's God's will," David answered, tears shimmering in his eyes.

"Well, I can't thank you enough. And, yes, let's go talk to Kristina," Dylan said, his nervousness causing beads of sweat to form on his forehead.

"Calm down. It's going to be okay," David said, remembering when he had proposed to Melony and feeling a little sympathy for Dylan. *At least I hadn't had to face Melony's dad the way that Dylan had been forced to face me.* That thought made David smile as he and his future son-in-law walked into the house.

Kristina glanced up. She heard them coming. She felt her heart start racing fear and excitement gripping her. What had they decided? Would she be going to Australia? She wondered. They opened the door and stepped inside as Kristina searched her dad's face for any signs. He smiled at her and looked over at Melony.

"Come on, honey. Dylan wants to talk to Kristina. Let's all go to the living room," he said, smiling as Melony whirled and gravy from the spoon in her hand flew all over Dylan.

Dylan gasped. *Ouch! That was hot*, he thought. *She's trying to kill me before I even have the chance to marry her daughter.*

He heard Kristina's quick intake of breath followed by running feet. He looked up to find her peering into his face.

Kristina gasped. Her mom did not just throw hot gravy all over her future husband. She couldn't have. Things like that didn't really happen. She had to go make sure he was all right. She run over to him and tried to tell by his face whether or not he was in pain. "Are you okay?" she asked, worry written all over her face. He looked down at her, and she caught her breath. His eyes were so beautiful. Such a rich dark brown. She blushed.

"I'm fine," he answered, smiling at her knowingly. "So, do I do in a pinch?" He grinned.

She felt tears well up in her eyes and start streaming down her face.

David and Melony looked at one another.

"What?" David mouthed to her.

"I haven't the slightest idea," she said back.

Dylan looked at her, knowing her answer would hold their future. He felt anticipation. He already knew what her answer was by the look on her face.

"Yes, yes, you do in a pinch," she answered, laughing and crying all at the same time.

"Good then," he said, grinning. "So now, my future wife, are you hungry?" He took the hand towel Kristina's grandmother handed him and wiped the gravy from his shirt.

"Yes, I am hungry," she responded, drying her tears and laughing. She ran to her mom and hugged her, and then ran to her dad. "I'm going to Australia!" she screamed. She heard Dylan laugh and turned to look at him. *He is so handsome*, she thought, gazing into his eyes.

"Yes, you are going to Australia," he said, smiling. "I take it you are excited?"

"Yes, I am so excited," she answered, grinning back. "Oh, and can I tell you something?"

He nodded. "Of course. We are getting married in a little while after all," he said, grinning.

David and Melony looked at one another. "What just happened?" he asked her, looking confused.

"I have no idea how, but somehow, he just asked your daughter to marry him, and she accepted," she told him, smiling.

"But how?" he asked.

Kristina glanced over at them and laughed. "Yesterday at the church, as Dylan was coming in, he ran into me and Megan. Somehow, Megan picked up on the fact that I thought he was handsome and asked me about it. Dylan heard her and decided he was curious about the answer. So he asked me if I thought he was handsome, and I said he would do in a pinch." Kristina finished up breathlessly.

Melony looked at David, and they smiled at one another. Kristina and Dylan hadn't even known each other twenty-four hours and already they shared a wonderful lasting memory.

Dylan cleared his throat, and everyone turned to look at him, but he had eyes only for Kristina. "So you think I'm handsome?" he asked, gazing at her.

"Nope," she responded laughingly. "I think you're absolutely gorgeous."

He smiled. He used to think that if a woman ever told him that, he would feel awkward, but he just felt happy. He looked into her eyes and smiled. "And I think you are beautiful. Now let's eat, I am starving," he said, turning toward the table.

David laughed. "Well, seems the boy has a two-track mind. First, woo his fiancée, and second, eat," he said. They all laughed and sat down.

EPILOGUE

The next day, Dylan stepped out of the small one-engine airplane and turned to help his wife down. He smiled as she came into view. Her beautiful blonde hair was blowing in the wind, and her smile lit up his heart. He smiled at her and watched as she got her first view of Australia. He had been terrified to get married, and he still was terrified of what was coming in the future. But he knew God would take care of them, all they had to do was trust.

I am here. I am finally here. Where I can help all those dying people, the ones that are lost and going to hell, and I can be one of those people who tell them about Jesus. Kristina glanced down at her husband. He was so handsome standing there, his black hair rising in the wind and his chocolate-brown eyes twinkling. God had truly blessed her. Fear still edged her happiness, but she knew God had a plan.

As she stepped down into her husband's waiting arms, she thought about the past few days and realized the pain was gone. She was doing something to help the people of Australia; she no longer felt helpless. She smiled as her husband put his arms tight around her. God had a plan. This whole time when she had doubted him, he had a plan.

Dylan closed his arms around his wife and rested his head on her shoulder. He closed his eyes. The pain of losing Matt was dimming. He was so happy. The hole that had been in his heart for so long was now full. They had a long way to go and a lot to learn, but he knew that God had a plan. Even when it seemed like there was nowhere to go. There was no way anything could get any better within the allotted time frame. Now he knew that was when God worked his miracles and made wonderful things happen. He raised his head upward toward the sky, feeling the warm Australian air glide over his face. He kept his eyes closed and breathed a prayer. "God, thank you for giving me this wonderful woman. Thank you for granting me patience to wait on the right one. I know I got impatient at the end, but I still married the one you had planned for me. God, after talking to her on the plane, I realize that up until yesterday, our hearts were bleeding and hurting. Thank you for healing hearts."